FINAL CHAPTER

A MEGAN MONTAIGNE MYSTERY

BOOKS by PAM STUCKY

FICTION

the Wishing Rock series (contemporary fiction)
(novels with recipes)
Letters from Wishing Rock
The Wishing Rock Theory of Life
The Tides of Wishing Rock

Balky Point Adventures (MG/YA sci-fi)
The Universes Inside the Lighthouse
The Secret of the Dark Galaxy Stone

Mystery
Death at Glacier Lake
Final Chapter: A Megan Montaigne Mystery

NONFICTION

the Pam on the Map travel series
(wit and wanderlust)
Pam on the Map: Iceland
Pam on the Map: Seattle Day Trips
Pam on the Map (Retrospective): Switzerland
Pam on the Map (Retrospective): Ireland

From the Wishing Rock Kitchens: Recipes from the Series

www.pamstucky.com
twitter.com/pamstucky
facebook.com/pamstuckyauthor
pinterest.com/pamstucky

FINAL CHAPTER

A MEGAN MONTAIGNE MYSTERY

PAM STUCKY

Wishing Rock Press

Copyright © 2018 Pam Stucky

Published in the United States by Wishing Rock Press.

Cover design by www.ebooklaunch.com.

ISBN (print): 978-1-940800-16-5
ISBN (ebook): 978-1-940800-17-2

www.wishingrockpress.com

for Agatha, who led the way

"To die of old age is a death rare, extraordinary, and singular, and, therefore, so much less natural than the others; 'tis the last and extremest sort of dying."

— *Michel de Montaigne, 1533–1592*

one

The river raced by with an indifferent confidence, coursing along on the path it had chosen. It was running unusually high, its silky surface moving like a sheet, masking the hidden treachery lurking just beneath.

"You don't realize how loud rivers can be until you live next to one, do you?" Megan Montaigne said. She'd been living in this apartment above the library for a few months now, but was sure she'd never tire of this view. Her apartment, along with this spectacular balcony, was a perk of her job. What was now a library had once been a mansion, a house far too big for the needs of just the library. As such, the library board had decided to convert the upper rooms to living quarters for the Library Director. That was Megan. She was grateful.

"I mean, not loud, really," Megan continued. "But nonstop. Not quiet. Peaceful, but in a different way." Below her, the waters of the Skagit River, in the northern part of Washington state, rushed by. The library was situated on a bump of land at a turn of the river, offering an expansive and uninterrupted

view. "The Skagit River," Megan said, shaking her head. "Someone called the other day and pronounced it wrong. I swear the
tourism people need to adopt my slogan. 'Skagit, Rhymes with
Gadget, More or Less.' Catchy, right?" She reached for a slice
of apple from the plate on the table between her and her guest,
topped it with a slice of sharp cheddar, and took a bite. "Thanks
so much for the snack," she said.

"It's the least I could do," smiled Romy Garrison, cozy and
content curled up in her Adirondack chair. Romy was better
known to her readers as Rosemary Grace Garrison—a name
that was splashed across the fifty-and-counting novels she'd
written over the past twenty-five years. "You're so nice to let me
stay here while my new hardwoods cure." A cool April evening
breeze blew a strand of her short blonde hair across her eyes,
and she absentmindedly brushed the lock away. "This construction has gone on twice as long as they told me it would. They
were supposed to be done before I moved in, but, that's the way
it goes, I guess." She leaned forward and twisted to the right,
squinting down the river at the land on the other side. "I wondered if I'd be able to see my house from here, but I guess not,"
she said, leaning back. "You're right, though. I had no idea. My
bedroom looks out over the river, and at night that white noise
just puts me right to sleep. I suppose you get used to it. The su-
surrus of the river. Susurration."

Megan smiled at the word and repeated it. "Susurration.
Yes, that's it. The whispering of the water. Such a good word.
I suppose that's why you're a writer," she said. Being around
the world-famous author still made her a little nervous. Romy's move to the tiny town of Emerson Falls had been the buzz
of the community for more than a year—as were her ongoing
construction woes. She was building her dream home on the
other side of the river, and construction was supposed to be
done months ago. Romy's original plan was to have the house

completed by September, at which point she would move in. As it happened, the building had been nowhere near finished in September. Finally, by January, it had been at least livable, and she'd chosen to exist within the chaos, hoping, she'd said, that her presence would speed things along.

At a recent library board meeting, the vice president had mentioned that Romy would soon need somewhere to stay for a few days while the fumes from the finish of the reclaimed wood floors dissipated. Without even thinking, Megan had blurted out, "The guest rooms at the library! She could stay there." Wanting to gain favor with the writer, the board immediately jumped on the idea. Before the meeting was over, Romy had been invited and the offer accepted.

If she was honest, Megan welcomed the company, despite the disruption of her own routine. At fourteen thousand square feet, the home was far too big for one person alone. What was now the library had originally been the preposterously large vacation retreat of Edison Finley Wright—and his now-ex-wife. To spite his ex, rumor had it, Edison had donated it to the community for its current use. The library board hadn't known what to do with the mansion at first. Emerson Falls was a small town, and even if you brought in books for the people in every town within a twenty-mile radius, the community library still didn't need such a huge space. After much discussion, the board had finally come up with a solution everyone loved: the main level would house the books and library activities, the lower level would be converted into conference rooms and other community gathering spaces, and the top floor would be remodeled as a living space for the Library Director.

"I'm still getting used to it," Megan said. "It's not too noisy here, which is good. One time, when we went to Hawaii, we stayed in a condo right on the water. I couldn't believe how loud the waves were. There we were, in paradise, and it turned out paradise roared. We kept the windows open at night, of course, and sometimes a big, crashing wave would actually wake me up. Never underestimate the power of water."

Romy's eyebrows lifted. "'We'?" she said. "Someone special?" She broke off a small piece of cheese and nibbled on it, her eyes sparkling with interest.

The light was growing dim as evening crept in. Megan looked up, wondering about the possibility of a sunset. She hesitated in answering Romy's question. It had been almost a year, and she had, more or less, "moved on." In her mind, the phrase always had quotation marks around it. What could it mean to "move on" from a person whose life had infused her own? She sighed. It was an innocent enough question. "Zeus. I mean, Luke. He went by Zeus. He was a river rafter. That's what they called him."

This news clearly delighted Romy. "Zeus! How did he get that name? Those are some big shoes."

Megan blinked. "Well, the river rafters, lots of them lead guided tours with people who come to see the bald eagles." She glanced at the treetops to see if any of the white-headed birds were present. "They had a sort of competition, not an official competition or anything, but they always competed to see whose boat could spot the most eagles during the rafting trips. Zeus always won. By far. He was the eagle whisperer." She smiled lightly at the memory. "His clients would come back glowing, raving about seeing dozens of eagles, fifty or seventy every trip. The girlfriend of one of the other guides was a Greek mythology buff. She told us that Zeus—the Greek god, that is, not Luke—had an eagle as a personal messenger and companion. *Aetos Dios*, the Eagle of Zeus. *Aetos Dios* was a golden eagle, not a bald eagle, but it was close enough. People started calling Luke Zeus, and the name stuck." She looked back at the cottonwoods lining the riverbank on the opposite side, knowing she was unlikely to see any of the birds, whether bald or golden.

Wrong time of day; wrong time of year. Still, she looked. Every time Megan saw an eagle in flight, her heart leapt, a little hopeless prayer that the sighting was meant just for her.

"What a fabulous nickname," said Romy. "Your Greek god is no longer in the picture, I take it?" She, too, was scanning the river for eagles, but her unpracticed eyes were less focused. Her powers of observation were strongest with humans.

Megan sighed internally. She hated this part. "No," she said. "He died."

Whoosh. Megan was used to it by now, the way speaking those words sucked the energy out of a space and stopped all conversation. The author let out a quick, hard breath. Her arm dropped and her fingertips gently touched the arm of the weathered Adirondack chair she was sitting in, the way she might have touched Megan, in comfort, if the two women had been closer either physically or emotionally, or both. "I'm so sorry. That's ... well, that's unbearable, I suppose. Do you want to talk about it?"

Normally, Megan would have said no. In fact, usually she did say no. "I'm fine" and "Oh, don't worry about me" had become a part of her regular vocabulary. Something about Romy, though, made Megan want to share. Or maybe it was the cloak of impending night, the susurration of the water washing away her inhibitions. "Yes," she said, "actually I do."

"I'm listening," said Romy, filling their wine glasses with the red blend she'd brought over when she first knocked on Megan's door earlier that evening. "Tell me what you need someone to hear."

Megan took a deep breath. She swirled the red wine in her glass and watched the tiny whirlpool chase the liquid up the sides and then settle again. "Zeus," she finally said, "Zeus was a good guy. Stubborn, but in a 'nothing and no one is going to stop me' kind of way. When he wanted something, he'd go for it. He doubted himself more than he'd ever let on. He always wanted to put on a strong show, but I saw the side he didn't let too many people see. The side of him that believed if he was ever weak, people would think he wasn't a real man. He was fiercely loyal and always had my back. He believed in me far more than I ever believed in myself. He was a free spirit, completely unconcerned with convention and society's rules. He was not the kind of guy I expected to fall in love with, but I did." A jolt of pain shot through her heart. She swirled the wine again, then took a sip.

"Sounds like a good guy," said Romy, echoing Megan. "I'm sorry I didn't get to meet him. How did he die, if you don't mind my asking?"

"Plane accident," Megan said after a moment, tucking her long, slightly wavy, dark brunette hair behind her ear. "He was trying to learn to fly. He wanted to surprise me. But he was always doing too much, working too hard, not getting enough rest. On his third time out solo, he fell asleep and crashed. The irony was not lost on me that the God of the Sky died in a plane crash."

"I'm so sorry," said Romy, and Megan could feel that she really was. "I can't imagine. How long ago?"

"About a year. It's okay. I mean, it's not okay, if I could change it I would, but …"

Romy's sudden silence was full and awkward. Megan looked up and saw a strange expression on Romy's face, intense and concentrated, like she was trying to remember something, or like she'd remembered something that unsettled her. "A plane crash?" she said, but the words seemed to be intended for herself.

The intensity was too much for Megan. What was Romy thinking about? Maybe she didn't want to know. "Enough about me," Megan said, shaking her head to dispel the memories. "Tell me about you."

"Well," said Romy. Eyes to the sky, she seemed to scroll

through a list of her life stories before speaking. "Well, I was married once, for many years."

Megan curled her lips around her teeth and pressed them together, a subconscious move telling her body: *say nothing.* Of course she knew Romy had been married. When word had first hit that Romy was moving to the area, the town gossips had dug up every scrap of data on her. Romy's life story became common currency. Everyone knew there was a divorce, too, but the reasons behind the split had never made it to the tabloids. "What happened?" Megan asked, then immediately regretted it. "I mean, sorry, I don't mean to pry. That's private."

Romy laughed and waved her hand in the air. "Oh, it's fine. It's in the past." By now the sunlight was beginning to fade; shadows were beginning to grow as night reclaimed the sky. "I was always wrong, and he was always right. That's what happened. It took me forever to realize that things were not always my fault, and I didn't actually have to apologize for everything I did that he didn't like." She stared deep into the wine for a long time, as if it carried all her memories. "Eventually I figured it out."

"What a jerk," Megan said. "I'm sorry."

"No, he's not a jerk," Romy said, shaking her head slowly, sadly. "That's what made it hard to leave. I always thought one day he'd learn to trust me enough to be vulnerable with me, but he couldn't. He wasn't a jerk. Just broken. I know he loved me. I just couldn't take on all his pain anymore. I couldn't bear the weight of his insecurity. Much of the time things were great, but every time we had a disagreement I ended up feeling like the world's biggest loser. I had to leave. Long overdue, but I had to leave."

Megan took this in. She'd been lucky with Zeus. He was strong, and had fierce opinions. But he'd known how to be soft, how to let his guard down, how to reach back when she reached out, how to say he was sorry. A bolt of pain went through her chest.

"I miss him," she said, forgetting Romy was not inside her brain with her, or maybe forgetting she wasn't alone.

Romy's eyes were soft. She nodded. "I miss Gus too. I still love him. He's not a bad person. I would go back in a minute if I didn't think it would wreck the shreds of self-confidence I've built up since I left. But he would never take me back. I think he still loves me, too, but he was furious when I left him. Public embarrassment and making him look like the bad guy and whatnot. I tried to keep it all neutral in the press, but he felt like I'd made him out to look awful. He just can't handle being held accountable for the consequences of his actions." She shook her head. "I'm sorry, you were saying you miss Zeus and I made it about me. I guess you made me feel safe. Tell me more about Zeus."

Megan smiled and hugged her knees to her chest. "No need to apologize."

And so as the night fell, Megan found herself spilling everything, all of it. Romy listened intently, eyes wide, her expression shifting subtly to show she caught the fine nuances of every tale, asking questions and coaxing out answers like a story whisperer, drawing out secrets like Rumpelstiltskin gathering straw.

"It's funny, isn't it, how life doesn't turn out at all like we think it's going to. But it manages to turn out okay in the end." Romy nudged Megan and winked. "I mean, Edison as your patron, that's not a bad thing, right? He's cute?"

The outside lights had come on, casting sharp shadows and throwing the night into even thicker darkness. "Edison Finley Wright?" said Megan, who thought of the man as three names, not just one. The opposite of Oprah or Elvis or Cher, Edison Finley Wright, in her mind, bore the weight of all his syllables. "Do you know Edison well?" Megan asked. A glimmer of mischief flitted past Romy's eyes, and as she often had before, Megan marveled at how people could read each other's emotions almost like they could read books. Was it something about the squint of Romy's eyes? The lift of an eyebrow? A twitch in the cheek from a quickly suppressed smile? It happened so fast there was no way Megan could catalog it, but yet somehow she knew: mischief. "Is there a story there between you and Edison?" she smiled.

"Oh, Edison," said Romy, her voice filled with glee. "He's dangerous."

"Dangerous?" said Megan. "How so?"

"All charm. You know him, right?"

"From the library board, yes," Megan said.

"Well then, you know. He, uh…" she coughed lightly and scratched her neck. "He came to one of my book launches once, friend of a friend, and he flirted with me over canapés and champagne. A man who can make you laugh, that's what he is. That's what you really want, isn't it? Maybe one day I'll give in and let him date me."

"Give in?" said Megan.

"He's asked me out a dozen times," said Romy. "I keep telling him no. I'm too busy with the house remodel and getting settled here to think about dating. He can wait. But," she laughed, "I have seen the way the local ladies look at him. Maybe if I wait too long, he'll be off the market." She looked inward for a few moments, then changed the subject. "So, tell me. What made you want to be a librarian? Did you always want to be one?"

Megan smiled. "It all started with Nancy Drew, to be honest. I couldn't get enough Nancy Drew. I used to have all the books, carefully cataloged in a notebook and shelved in order. Foreshadowing, I'd say. You must have read her, too?"

"She's why I write mysteries," Romy beamed. "I loved that old strawberry blonde."

"I read voraciously as a kid. And one day, I realized that in books, everything is possible." Megan pictured in her mind the library beneath them, its rows upon rows of books. "You know how science fiction movies sometimes have mad scientists who keep endless jars of brains in some secret back room? Well, if you think about it, what you have down there—" she inclined her head in the direction of the library "—is a room full of brains. Every book is a piece of someone's brain. When I read a book, I'm basically reading someone's mind. Not their thoughts exactly, but you get an idea of their worldview, or at the very least, you get an idea of their understanding of humans. When I was a kid, it felt like that helped. I could understand the characters in books because I knew their motives. Books helped me figure people out." She laughed. "I guess. Or maybe they're just a good escape. But, I mean, libraries include everything we can think of in the universe. All possibilities. If someone has imagined it, it's in a library. That's pretty amazing."

A smile crept across Romy's face. "A room full of brains," she said. "I love that. That's perfect." A sudden thought popped her eyes wide open. "Say, you should come to my housewarming party. Next week. The house is mostly done. It's time to celebrate."

"I'd be honored," Megan said. She wrapped her arms around herself and gazed out at the reflections of lights shimmering on the river. The past year had been the worst of her life. But now, here she was, on top of a mansion sharing deep thoughts with one of the nation's best writers, sipping wine as the moon rose up over the trees. The thought made her smile. For a moment, she felt hope again. She reached out to that hope and held it tight.

two

"What's for lunch?" Megan said brightly as she walked into Rae's Pub, a favorite local hangout. Rae Norris, the owner and a master chef—at least as far as standard bar and grill fare went—could never be bothered to print up an actual menu, but the food was so good that no one cared. Hungry patrons simply walked in and ate what she was serving that day, just like they'd eat whatever their moms served when they were kids. Megan settled herself onto a seat at the bar next to Officer Max Coleman, the Deputy whose beat included Emerson Falls. "Is it burgers?" Megan said, noticing a drop of ketchup and some breadcrumbs on Max's otherwise empty plate. "I hope it's burgers." Rae's burgers were legendary: juicy, always cooked to perfection (grilled to a sweet spot between medium and medium rare, because that's how you liked it whether you knew it or not), topped with sautéed onions, shredded lettuce, fresh tomato, a sharp cheddar, and a secret tangy sauce that many had tried to replicate, but none had succeeded.

Max gave Megan a nod of welcome. "It's burgers," he smiled,

flashing a row of perfect white teeth. Max had become a part of the local police force less than a year prior, and Megan had often wondered why he hadn't pursued modeling. The floppy, slightly curly black hair; the brown eyes that penetrated your soul; the physique that could be on a Police Men of the Skagit Valley Calendar, should someone ever be inclined to make one. Max was camera-ready. Surely, Megan thought, surely one day she'd find out he had a fatal flaw of some sort: he kept dozens of kittens locked up in an attic cage with no food, or he stole presents from children with cancer, or he insisted on putting cilantro into every dish he made. Megan hated cilantro.

"Yes," Megan said, pumping her arm to show her enthusiasm about the burgers. "So what's new, Max?" she said, as Max reached over the counter to grab a pitcher and pour her a glass of water.

"K9," said Max, handing her the glass.

"Canine? Dogs?" said Megan. She took a sip of the water. "Ahhhh," she said. "Water."

Max gave her a funny look and smiled, dimples denting his cheeks. "Water is good. And K9. Letter K, number nine, not c-a-n-i-n-e. A police dog. I've been asking since I started if I could get one. I'm out on my own all the time, patrolling this whole area by myself. Seems only right I should have a K9 companion to keep me company while I chase down the bad guys."

This probably negated the possibility that he had kittens locked up in the attic. "That seems fair," said Megan. "Good for back-up and whatnot. When will you find out?"

"Not sure," he said. "But probably soon. I always assume good things are going to happen soon." He smiled again, and Megan imagined a sparkling gleam bouncing off his teeth.

She tilted her head to ask him a very serious question. "Max, how do you feel about cilantro?"

"Cilantro?" he said, puzzled but willing to go along with the line of questioning. "I love it. I make this great salsa, cilantro salsa. It's delicious on everything. Cilantro's amazing." He raised an eyebrow: *why are we talking about cilantro?*

"Cilantro is gross," Megan said, feeling slightly smug. At last. A fault.

The door that led to the kitchen swung open and Rae emerged carrying a plate of fries and a burger, which she set unceremoniously in front of Megan. "Heard you come in," she said. "Burgers today." She winked. "Eat up."

"You're the best, Rae," said Megan, cutting the enormous burger in half. "How's things here?"

"Woke up to another day, can't complain," said Rae. "Not as fancy as living in a mansion, going to celebrity open houses and such, but still, can't complain." She looked at Megan, the question in her eyes indicating she was awaiting some information.

"Ah," said Megan. "You must have talked to Lily." Lily Bell was one of Megan's closest friends, and the only person Megan had told about being invited to Romy's housewarming. Lily was also the owner of a local B&B, with a catering business on the side, and she had been hired to cater Romy's party. As soon as Romy had packed up and returned to her own home, Megan had called Lily for advice on what a person should wear to such an event. Lily had promised to come over later to dig through Megan's closet to find just the right outfit.

"Can't believe you told Lily but didn't tell old Rae," said Rae, feigning offense. "How'd you get yourself invited to that?"

"While Romy was staying at the library"—Megan felt odd calling referring to it as "my house"—"we had a lot of great conversations. She's such a good listener. Like, you feel really *heard.* I guess we just bonded. She invited me. I couldn't say no!"

"I'm a good listener," said Rae. "Aren't I, Max?"

"What?" said Max, eyes wide and innocent. "Sorry, I wasn't listening." His dimples revealed his lie.

"You are a no-good person," said Rae, swatting at him with a dishtowel she pulled off her shoulder. "Go on, get out of here, go save the town from some criminal."

Max laughed, a hearty laugh that came from his gut. He dropped a ten-dollar bill on the counter. "I do have to be getting back to work. Keep the change." He winked, got up, and left.

"'Keep the change,'" Rae mimicked. "All two dollars of it, what a gent." But her smile showed her fondness for the police officer. Even if he hadn't been around long, he already fit right in. "You and Lily gotta report back on that house, then," she said to Megan. "Can't believe old Rae didn't get an invite."

"I can't believe it, Rae," Megan affirmed solemnly. "You're the backbone of Emerson Falls."

"That's right," said Rae. "You tell that writer that when you see her next. Party's Sunday?"

"Sunday," said Megan. "We will come back with all the scoop. I promise."

"What's she like, the author? She's come in here a couple of times but she sits at a table." Sitting at a table at Rae's was a sure way to identify oneself as an outsider. If they were eating alone, locals sat at the bar, unless it was full. Tables were for tourists, passing through on their way to the mountains.

"She's nice," said Megan. "I really liked her. Maybe I'll see if she wants to do an author event at the library. Honestly, I'd sort of assumed she'd be … I don't know, too good for us. But she was down to earth. Just like a normal person."

"Doesn't her ex-husband live over by Concrete?" said Rae. "I'm sure I heard that. He bought up some land near the lake and started building there shortly after Romy started building here."

"Could be," said Megan, shrugging. "You hear a lot more gossip than I do."

"That's because I'm such a good listener," Rae said over her

shoulder, twirling her dishtowel in the air as she headed back
to the kitchen.

* * *

Sunday morning, Megan was awake early. Had a noise startled her awake, or was it just the growing light, the lengthening
days, that alerted her body it was time to get up? Regardless, she
stretched and got out of bed. Giant windows and French doors
on the river side of her bedroom beckoned to her. These doors
led to a second, smaller deck than the one where she and Romy
had sat talking the other night.

The April air was crisp and the sun was weak, but Megan
thought that if she was lucky enough to have a bedroom balcony with this magnificent view, she should use it. Padding into
the kitchen, she sighed with contentment. "Green tea today, I
think," she said to the kitchen, as she poked through her tea
choices. When she was alone, Megan had a tendency to talk
out loud, to herself, to the room, to the river, to her thoughts,
to whatever was occupying her mind. She put the electric kettle
on to boil and dropped a tea bag into her favorite mug, a bright
yellow oversized ceramic piece with rounded sides.

Once the tea was ready, she headed out onto the bedroom
balcony to greet the morning. "Good morning, river," she said
as she settled into her favorite Adirondack chair, painted a crisp
white.

She sipped her tea slowly, savoring the beam of sunshine
that had broken through the clouds to welcome her. The river
rushed by, the sound of it filling her as she contemplated the
natural force. "Never the same river twice," Megan said under
her breath. She thought about the saying. The river itself was the
same, but every drop today was a different drop than every drop
a year ago. She watched the water as it danced and sidestepped

around rocks, twirling twigs and leaves in its path to wherever it might end up, only to be replaced by the water behind it in an endless cycle of nature.

She looked to the treetops. Come winter, the trees would be filled again with dozens of eagles in some places, perched on high, looking down into the river, watching the salmon spawning grounds for their unsuspecting prey. Megan hoped she might spot a nest; that there might be new eagle friends in her own territory that she could watch every day from her own perch.

Her heart dropped momentarily as she thought of Zeus. She sighed heavily.

"I know you're still here," she said to the treetops. A part of her brain held her hopes in suspension, waiting for an eagle to appear that surely would be a sign.

None came.

A cloud covered the sun again. Megan looked at her watch. Eight o'clock. The housewarming wasn't until one. She settled into her chair and breathed.

three

At the last minute, Megan realized she'd forgotten about a house-warming gift for Romy. Houseplant? Bottle of wine? Gourmet gift food? She dug through her cupboards, found a red blend from a local winery, and decided that would be good enough. Dressed in a forest green pencil skirt and a white knit top, her long hair curled into loose waves for the event, she hopped in her car and headed to the party.

Romy's new home was on the other side of the river, near a side channel that broke off from the main river and re-joined about a mile downstream. Though Romy's house was very close to the library as the eagle flies, to get there Megan had to drive several miles west to a bridge, across the river, and then back east to Romy's property. GPS was sometimes sketchy in this area, but Romy had emailed precise directions to all the invitees. At the final turn into the driveway, someone had tied a festive bouquet of balloons. The driveway was long but ungated. A handful of construction trailers still lined the way, and a por-

Pam Stucky

table outhouse sat, green and garish, a few dozen feet outside the front door.

As Megan was trying to figure out where to park, she saw a man in black jeans and a crisp white button-down shirt running toward her.

"Kevin!" Megan exclaimed as the man approached her rolled-down window. "What are you doing here?" Kevin had been one of Zeus's friends, a fellow river rafter, and one of the more talented ones.

"Some extra cash," Kevin said, leaning into Megan's window, rubbing his blond buzz cut. "My girlfriend is Romy's assistant. She got me a job doing valet parking today."

Megan couldn't believe she'd missed the news that Kevin was dating someone who worked for Romy, but then since Zeus died, she'd lost touch with the river rafting group. "It's good to see you," she said, a little wistfully. "Will you come join the party so we can catch up?" Zeus's death had been especially hard on the fellow rafter. As another side job, Kevin had worked at the hangar where Zeus had been learning to fly. After Zeus died, Kevin had quit that job, saying it was too painful to return.

Kevin straightened up. "Not sure I'll have time, but I'll try. Let me park your car for you. But yeah, we should catch up." His smile was forced and sad.

Megan felt bad for not having reached out to the young man more. She'd been Zeus's fiancé, sure, but that didn't mean she'd been the only one who had cared about him. She promised herself she'd make an effort to see Kevin soon. Grabbing her purse and the wine from the passenger seat, Megan stepped out of the car and handed Kevin her keys. "Thanks. It's really good to see you, Kevin. Come inside when you can, okay? You need to tell me what's up with your life."

His answer was a salute, which seemed more like a non-commitment than a reply. Megan let it slide, and headed to the front door.

Much to Megan's surprise Romy opened the door herself, wearing a cocktail dress in a dark dusty rose. "My first guest!" Romy exclaimed, her arms flung wide in welcome. "Come in, come in!"

Megan blushed as she looked at her watch. Just barely one o'clock. She'd overestimated how long it would take her to get there, and now she was embarrassingly right on time. Who arrived at a party right on time? "I do, that's who." Megan whispered the words, not realizing until they came out that she was speaking out loud.

"What?" said Romy, linking arms with Megan and leading her inside.

"Sorry, I didn't mean to be so early," Megan said. She handed Romy the wine. "Wine," she said.

Romy looked over the bottle with delight. "I've been meaning to check out this winery! Thank you!" She set the bottle on a table. "Don't worry a bit. I like punctuality. If I say a party starts at one, then the party starts at one! Even if it's just you and me. This gives me a chance to show you around the house and give you my full attention." She led Megan through the various rooms of the house, pointing out her favorite features in each: the crown molding in one, a tiled fireplace in another, and the newly cured hardwood floors that had been the reason she'd needed to stay with Megan in the first place. Finally they got to the library. Megan gasped in delight at the shelves of books lining every wall, and the two short, freestanding shelves in the middle of the room. A chaise longue and an overstuffed chair sat on either side of a fireplace. Wide windows were outfitted with thick-cushioned window seats, just waiting for a reader and perhaps a cat to curl up during a rainstorm.

Romy's eyes danced. "I have to show you something," she said. She dropped her arm from Megan's elbow and grasped her hand, an excited child leading her friend to a treasure. "Over here," she said, pointing at a shelf of books near the fireplace.

Without having to be told what she was looking at, Megan instantly recognized the aged blue cloth spines of three rows of books. "Nancy Drew!" she exclaimed, her voice tinged with awe. "First editions?" She reached out and gently caressed the covers. "May I?" she said, looking at Romy.

"Of course! Yes, Nancy Drew! You mentioned the other day that you're a fan, too. I had to show you. Not all first editions, but many. Others are just from the original series. But …" With great care, she pulled a book off a shelf, one of the few books that still had an intact dust cover. "*The Secret of the Old Clock*, first printing, 1930. This was a gift from my agent when my fiftieth book was released. She spent two years looking for it, she told me! Too bad you won't meet her. She's on maternity leave. My fill-in agent is coming today, though," she said. Her pursed lips suggested she was not her temporary agent's biggest fan.

"This is incredible," said Megan, flipping reverently through the book. She handed it back to Romy, scared to hold it for too long. Her eyes gleamed as she gazed around the room. "It's all so beautiful. You must be thrilled," said Megan.

"Thrilled that the renovations and construction are almost over," said Romy. "Never again! Now, let me show you to the back. Where all the action is! We lucked out on a nice, sunny day, so we're having the party outside." She led Megan out a set of French doors onto a patio where catering staff were busily milling about, arranging platters of appetizers on one long table in the middle and setting out the final centerpieces on round tables covered with crisp white linen.

Megan saw her friend Lily at the main table and waved.

"You know Lily?" said Romy. A woman approached them

with a tray of cocktails and wine. Romy picked a glass of red from the tray, and Megan selected what looked like it might be a margarita on the rocks.

"One of my closest friends," said Megan. "You were smart to hire her. She's the best." She looked around the vast, impeccably landscaped lawn. "Again, all so beautiful. Well done."

"I can't take the credit. I signed the checks; that's about it. But thank you. It's becoming the sanctuary I wanted. I can't wait for the workers and that porta-potty to be gone, though, that's for sure!" She continued to lead Megan around the parameter of the house, pointing out her favorite plants, a decorative bench, and in the distance, a teak lattice structure, from which a very large hammock hung. As they neared the side of the house, a large pool came into view, out toward the edge of the property.

Megan noticed that Romy's expression changed on seeing the pool. "Did they get the construction on the pool wrong?" she asked.

Romy straightened her back. "This pool is my cross to bear," she said. "I shouldn't have had it put in, but I did. It was an emotional decision, not a logical one." She took a sip of her wine. With her other arm still linked in Megan's, she pivoted them around to return to the party area. "Gus used to swim," Romy said. "Still does, I guess. I swam a bit, too. I like it but I was never any good. I had the contractor put in a pool because … well, I suppose because old habits die hard."

She trailed off, her mind lost in her memories. Megan wondered if the old habit Romy was referring to was swimming, or Gus.

"Rooooooooommmmmyyyyy!" A woman's high-pitched voice cut through the air. Romy and Megan turned to see where the voice was coming from. A lean, lanky woman was approaching them, her wild and curly hair, a mix of light and dark blonde, flying out as if she'd just shuffled across the carpet in her wool socks and held a balloon to her head. A bright red scarf was tied in complex knots around her neck, standing out in stark contrast to the long-sleeved black sheath dress beneath it. Her heels were precariously high and too sharp for walking on grass, which was causing the woman to inch awkwardly forward on her toes. Behind her trailed a shorter man, dressed in a gray twill suit and thick-rimmed glasses.

"Oh, it's the fill-in agent," said Romy under her breath, just loud enough for Megan to hear, before plastering on a smile. "Emlyn!" she called out to the woman. "So good of you to come! I hope the trip was all right?"

Emlyn stopped and balanced her weight over her toes. She quickly seized a glass of red wine off a tray as a server walked by. The man with her looked down his nose at the offerings and asked the server if she could get him a Rusty Nail. "Do you know what that is?" he said. With a slightly annoyed nod, the server clipped off toward the bar.

"Megan Montaigne," said Romy, holding out her hands toward Megan as though she were serving up a prize on a game show, "this is my temporary agent, Emlyn Cooper." She moved her hands to indicate the woman in heels. "And Emlyn, I'm afraid I'm at a loss. This is …?" She nodded at the man in the twill.

Emlyn held out her hand, smooth and perfectly manicured, to shake Megan's. "This is my husband, Baz Scurlock."

"Sherlock?" said Megan, who had misheard.

"Scurlock," said Baz sourly. It seemed he had heard it before and was not amused.

"Oh, I'm sorry," said Megan. "Nice to meet you both."

Emlyn instantly dismissed Megan and talked breathlessly to Romy. "The flight was unpleasant at best. JFK, you know, always a madhouse, and the first class line didn't have enough staff. I had to wait! Can you imagine? But, such as it was, we got here last night and had a lovely cocktail downtown in Seattle at the top of that Smith Tower, have you been? At the speakeasy? Charming, almost nice enough that it could be out east. Maybe not New York but at least Philadelphia. And the drive up here! What a rural place you live in!" It was clear that "rural" was the kindest word Emlyn could think of for the area.

Megan caught Romy's eye and mouthed that she was going to go find Lily. "Nice to meet you both," she said to Emlyn and Baz, and she headed over to the food. She looked back over her shoulder at the trio she was leaving, and it seemed only Romy noticed she had left. Megan was glad she'd offered up a room at her library, giving her a chance to get to know the author as a person. Romy was the kind of woman whose good heart would help her age gracefully. Her short, straight hair, now in a layered bob that curved in delicately to frame her chin, would, of course, turn to a snowy white rather than a muddy gray. The wrinkles she acquired, already starting to show at the corners of her eyes, would grant her the visage of venerable wisdom rather than withered dotage. Her posture would remain regal and her mind sharp, all the way through her nineties. Romy saw Megan looking at her and winked ever so slightly, a tiny smile curling the corner of her lip.

Lily saw Megan coming and was beaming with delight before her friend reached the table. Being in Lily's presence always felt like coming home for Megan; like exhaling after holding her breath too long. Megan and Lily had met shortly after Megan had moved to Emerson Falls, and had instantly recognized each other as long-lost friends.

"Lily Bell!" said Megan with joy. She loved the combination of Lily's first and last names and often used them both.

Lily reached out to give Megan a gentle hug, careful not to contaminate her hands in their food-grade latex-free gloves. Her shoulder-length auburn hair was carefully gathered at the nape of her neck with a wide gold clip, and a crisp white apron covered her sleek knee-length periwinkle dress. Unlike Emlyn, Lily had chosen more practical, almost-flat heels in a coordinating but slightly darker blue. "How are you? I'm so glad you're here!" Lily said as she went back to arranging the food trays. Other guests had started to arrive for the party, and Lily was keeping a watchful eye on the platters of delectable appetizers to make sure none was empty.

"Look at you, biggest party in Emerson Falls of the year, and here you are in charge!" Megan said.

Lily brushed off the praise with a giant smile and a wave of her gloved hand. "You are so silly. It's just hors d'oeuvres. And it doesn't take much to make it the biggest party in Emerson Falls! But look over here! Look at this! This is amazing!" She led Megan to the end of the very long table where several large cakes lay, enticing the eyes with their intricate decorations. One was a perfect replica of Romy's new house; around it were several smaller, rectangular cakes, each decorated in an exact likeness of the covers of Romy's most popular books.

"Wow," said Megan. "Did you make these? These are incredible!" She leaned in for a closer look at the cakes with the book covers. The reproductions were precise, down to the tiniest details, but the work had all been painstakingly done by hand.

"No, Courtney did." She looked around trying to find the woman she was referring to. "Romy's assistant. Have you met her?"

Megan looked around, too, though she had no idea who she was looking for. "I haven't, but Kevin mentioned that he's dating Romy's assistant. Same person?" she said. The yard was starting to fill up with people, most of whom were strangers to Megan, but some she knew from town.

"Yes, that's the one," said Lily. "Average height, long blonde hair, not a thing out of place," Lily said, seemingly oblivious to the fact that aside from the hair color, a person could describe

Lily the same way. She squinted into the crowd. "I can't see her. Maybe she's inside. Anyway, she lives out in Rockport. Moved there when Romy moved here. As it turns out, she's an amazing graphic designer and artist. Can you believe she did that freehand?" she said, indicating the cakes. "That's talent."

"Well, sure," said Megan, "But not like making enough appetizers to feed an army! No wonder I haven't seen you for so long. You've been busy! Are you managing with the B&B too?"

Lily sighed heavily but without losing her smile. "Steve's been pitching in big time. I'd be lost without him. He's been doing almost everything this last week," she said. Steve Bell was her husband of fifteen years; they'd met in grade school and married the day after they'd graduated from the same college. "Hopefully he's got it all together. Romy's agent is staying with us tonight."

"Emlyn?" Megan said. "I just met her. And her husband. *Temporary* agent, I think Romy would tell you. She seems … well, I think she might think our little town is not quite up to par." Megan scanned the crowd for the woman in black with the red scarf, and found her still plastered at Romy's side. A look at Lily's face told Megan that tomorrow morning, whatever Lily cooked up for breakfast, she was going to make sure it was going to be the best thing Emlyn had ever tasted. Unlike Megan, Lily was born and raised in this area. Her hometown loyalty was fierce.

"Two o'clock," said Lily suddenly, her eyes darting to her right, Megan's left.

"What?" said Megan, but before Lily could explain, Megan felt a warm hand on her upper arm, a gentle but confident touch.

"Megan! Megan Montaigne!" Edison said, his smile bright, his presence strong.

"Edison! Edison Finley Wright!" Megan replied, seeing the library's patron saint standing by her side. For a moment, as Edison's hand lingered on her arm, her thoughts lingered there with it. She was just starting to feel ready to date again. Edison was a handsome man. He was far more of an extrovert than she, but that would be a good balance, wouldn't it? Zeus had been an extrovert, too. She tried to remember if she knew Edison's age. Forty-something, which wasn't too old, really, for her late-thirty-something. His two kids were grown, one in high school and one just starting college, so there would be no diapers for a step-mother … Megan caught herself before almost whispering out loud: "Slow down, Megan, slow down."

"Megan, I can't tell you how grateful I am you put Romy up in the house," Edison said. He dropped his hand, but Megan's shoulder tingled with residual heat. "How's the old monstrosity working out for you?" On seeing the look on Megan's face, he clarified. "The mansion. It was always a monstrosity. It was my ex's idea to build that thing. She always wanted the biggest everything. She also is the type who can't stand if other people have things she can't have, which is why I gave the house away. It was my greatest act of compassion, I think." His face was serious but his eyes twinkled with self-amusement, and with something else that Megan couldn't identify.

"Your generosity is greatly appreciated," said Megan. "I appreciate it. The library and the apartments are perfect. I couldn't be more grateful."

"Now, now, now," said Edison, stopping her before she stumbled into a valley of platitudes. "You're welcome. Least I could do for such a fine town. I'm a fan of books. Speaking of which, have you seen Romy?" His green-blue eyes scanned the growing crowd.

Megan looked for a dark black dress and a bright red scarf, and quickly found Emlyn. Sure enough, she was still next to Romy, hanging on her every word while trying to look aloof and indifferent. "There," Megan said, pointing.

"Ah, with the agent and Courtney," Edison said. "Thanks." He patted Megan's shoulder again and nodded at Lily. "Great food, well done, Lily. Megan, I'll see you later," he said, and was off at a trot to see the hostess. When he reached Romy, his hand didn't go to her shoulder but instead to the small of her back. Megan felt a pang of jealousy as Romy's arm reached around Edison's waist and she briefly dipped her head onto his shoulder.

"Well," said Megan, not realizing Lily had been watching her watch the episode unfold.

"Hmmm?" said Lily.

"Nothing," said Megan. "Romy told me Edison was interested in her, but she didn't say she was interested in him. Sometimes … sometimes I feel really ready to have someone in my life again." She sighed.

"You will," said Lily. "When the time is right."

Megan hoped so, which somewhat surprised her. Maybe she would be ready one day, after all. But she knew now was not a time Lily could put on the best friend hat. They would have time to talk about all those hopes and woes later. She looked around again at the still-growing crowd. "Who are all these people? Do you know?"

"Lots of literary people up from Seattle, I think," Lily said. "Fellow authors. Wanna-be authors. Friends from out of town. I have no idea."

"So that's Courtney?" Megan said, looking again at the woman who was now talking to Emlyn, Romy's attention having been captured by Edison. "Kevin's girlfriend?" The woman was polished, sleek. Tailored form-fitting suit, looking more like a New York CEO than a personal assistant. Even from a distance she looked standoffish and cold. And yet, she and Emlyn seemed to be engaged in easy conversation. "Like attracts like, I guess," Megan said.

"That's her," said Lily, committing herself to no opinion on the subject matter. "We'll chat later," she said with a wink.

"How late are you here?" Megan asked. She suddenly felt like heading home to curl up with a good book.

"As long as it takes to clean up. I suspect the party might go late. Want me to come by after?"

"No, I'll probably be in bed early," said Megan, knowing that all this socializing would leave her exhausted. "I'll check in with you tomorrow." She grabbed another glass of wine off a passing tray, and left Lily to her work.

For a break from the small talk, Megan took herself on a tour of Romy's estate, this time self-guided. The rambling house itself was large but not obscenely so; nothing like the behemoth Edison Finley Wright's wife had created. Exterior walls painted in shades of beige with crisp off-white trimmings blended in with the tall cottonwoods that surrounded the grounds. The small lawn on the south side of the house still bore evidence of having been planted in pre-grown mats of grass, but with the spring rains, the seams were growing together nicely. At this point in the Skagit River's journey, for a short distance it coursed south to north rather than east to west. Although the front of the house faced the road to the west, the wide and deep back yard, on the river side, was the true focal point, and that was where everyone had gathered. The pool Romy had expressed such reservations about ran along the north side of the house and into the edge of the back yard, tucked in at the perimeter of the lot by the forest. Megan saw now that there was a small hot tub, too, close to the river with a perfect view of the mountains. She could imagine sitting out here on a warm summer's evening, listening to the owls as they welcomed the night, the sound of the river tumbling over rocks, the rustle of the wind high in the trees. The library was grand, but the home Romy had built somehow managed to be cozy as well. Maybe Megan would make some suggestions to Edison about how they might improve the library grounds. For the patrons, of course. For the patrons.

"Quite a place, eh?" said a voice behind Megan, making her jump. She turned and saw Edison there, as if she'd conjured him up out of her imagination.

Megan looked up at the trees over the pool. "It's a gorgeous setting. But the pool boy is going to have a full-time job keeping this thing clean." A few leaves were already floating on the surface, though Megan guessed Romy had had it cleaned for the party.

"Romy probably likes the pool boy," said Edison with a mischievous smile and a twinkle in his eye. "Maybe she did that by design."

Megan laughed. "I always forget how pretty this side of the river is. It's so different from the north side. Quieter. I think of the south side as the cottonwood side and the north side as the evergreen side, but I know that's not completely true." She paused. Did Edison know who Zeus was? Probably, but she wasn't sure. She'd wanted to say how she used to rely on Zeus to tell her what she needed to know about nature: no, those weren't alders; they were cottonwoods, for example. That was one of the earliest lessons. Or how you could tell a Douglas fir by its bottlebrush needles, sticking out on all sides, and its thick, furrowed bark. And of course the fact that it's not a true fir at all; unlike true firs, he had told her, the cones of Douglas firs hang down from their branches rather than standing up. But Megan's favorite trees, once she knew what they were, were the cedars, mostly Western Red Cedars in this area. She could instantly recognize them from their flat, scaly leaves and their unmistakable, stringy bark. Zeus had joked that Megan liked cedars because they were tidy and unambiguous. Megan would never acknowledge it, but there was something about the organized, calm look of cedars that appealed to her. That and their scent. The thought of it now made Megan wish for a hike out through the park by Emerson Falls. Maybe tomorrow.

"It's beautiful, for sure," said Edison. "If the ex-wife had bothered to look beyond the first thing she saw, we might have ended up on this side." His face clouded with memories.

"The library setting is perfect where it is," said Megan. "I can't believe you were willing to give it up. I mean, of course we're all grateful. But it's an amazing house, and amazing grounds."

Edison's nose twitched. "If those walls ever start to talk, you'll understand," he said, and he walked away.

* * *

After a few hours, Megan decided she'd put in enough time at the party. She'd talked to numerous authors of varying obscurity, many of whom had shoved business cards or bookmarks into her hands asking that she make sure her library stocked their books. She'd found herself standing again next to Emlyn, and listened for a short time to a monologue about how the west coast could never match the east coast in sophistication, prestige, beauty, class of people, driving ability, weather, public transportation, bagels, food in general … and by then Megan stopped listening but she assumed the list included smartness of babies and the talent of dogs and everything else under the sun (which of course was sure to be better on the east coast, as well). Megan chatted for a while with Lily again, and then decided it was time to go.

Her goodbye to Romy was brief. Always the way it was with the center of attention, Megan thought. Pulled in so many directions by so many people; never time to devote to just one person. Megan hoped they would have a chance to chat again soon. "Remember to plan Romy's author visit to the library," she muttered to herself as she took a final look around the gorgeous grounds, sneaking in to admire Romy's library one more time before heading out. Kevin quickly got her car for her, and after a brief hug, she left.

When she got back to the library, the peace of the river called to her. Megan ran upstairs to change into jeans and a sweater, then headed back outside, carrying a screw-top bottle of wine and no glass to go with it. She walked to the river along a path that led from the library down to what was meant to serve as a reading area. The area had been leveled and covered in crushed stone; a few benches, tables, and chairs were placed strategically to give the best view. Megan sat in her favorite chair and watched the river flow by. The people she'd met at the party had been interesting, but she was glad for some time alone.

As she tilted the bottle of wine to her lips, Megan guessed that Emlyn would not approve. Surely only west coast cretins drank directly from the bottle. This idea made the wine taste all the better, Megan thought with a smile. She took a swig and wiped her mouth with the back of her hand.

A few bright stars were just starting to make their appearance in the sky. Probably planets, thought Megan, wondering idly where Venus might be at the moment. Maybe, she thought, maybe with this halcyon location and this expansive view of the sky, the library should invest in telescopes. Night sky parties. Local astronomers mingling with romantic starry-eyed stargazers. Of course the library wouldn't have funding for it, but maybe Edison …

Edison's comment suddenly sprang to her mind. If the walls of the mansion could talk … what had he meant by that? It didn't matter. It was her turn, now, to build a life here. Strange, she thought, how many lives might be built on the same space, over the course of time. And how many might be torn apart.

four

"Good morning, bedroom," Megan said groggily as she opened her eyes and stretched. The morning was gray and cold. Having no neighbors who could peek into her room from the other side of the river, she'd taken to what felt like an exquisite luxury: sleeping with the curtains open. The windows were enormous, and it felt a bit like sleeping outside—without the bugs. When the moon was in the right position, Megan could watch it rise up over the treetops in its bright, looming silence. Its presence was mesmerizing; gazing on it felt like having a conversation in a language she couldn't quite understand. Like it had something to tell her, but it was expecting her to figure it out for herself.

Leaving the curtains open also meant the daylight acted as a natural alarm clock, whether she'd wanted one or not. It was just after six. Megan would have happily slept longer, but her brain said the sun was up and it was time to be awake.

"Fine," she said to the room. "I'll get up."

Despite the physical magnificence of the library, the county, which ran the library, did not have the funds to keep it open nine to five every day of the week. The best they could manage was weekday afternoons, extended to eight in the evening on Wednesdays. This meant Megan had her mornings free. Still, feeling indebted to the library foundation that allowed her to live rent-free in these quarters, she tried to spend some time each morning working to improve the library as she could. After a leisurely breakfast, she got dressed and headed to the public part of the building to assess where she would focus her energy for the day.

Though many changes had been made to the building to convert it into a library, it wasn't hard to see the original home underneath. Some people thought of Edison's donation as an example of exemplary charity. Others were certain it was nothing more than a tax write-off. Many thought Edison had given it away purely to spite his now ex-wife, who, rumor had it, loved the place more than she had ever loved Edison. Megan was undecided, though. And, really, it didn't matter. The building was now home.

The great room of the main floor now housed the library. What was once a large bedroom was now the library's back rooms and offices. The kitchen and dining room had been converted into a large staff area and lunchroom. On the opposite side of the main floor lay an extravagant four-car garage, which, at some point, given the right incentive and funding, might be converted into a small village theater.

The lower level had no windows at the front of the house, where the walls met up with rock, but the back side of the building opened up to a grand view of the river. This level had been converted into large spaces that could be rented at modest prices for meetings, conventions, parties, receptions, lectures, and the like. A man named Owen Scott managed the rentals from an office on the lower level that had once been a downstairs kitchen.

And the upstairs, of course, was the best part. The upstairs was now Megan's home. The master suite and sitting area, complete with fireplace, as well as the luxurious bathroom with a two-person bathtub and two-person shower, had remained as built. An extra bedroom suite and upstairs laundry area had been converted into a kitchen, living room, and dining room, and the vast walk-in closet had become a small office. The balconies that Megan treasured had also been part of the original design.

A bridge between the master suite on Megan's side, above the library offices, and more bedrooms on the other side allowed each to be locked off as separate apartments. The bedrooms on the other side had been adapted slightly to add tiny kitchenettes, with microwaves and mini-refrigerators, but any guests would also be welcome to use the full kitchen area in the staff lounge downstairs. Megan could house her own visitors in the spare suites, or visiting authors or other library guests could be put up there, as well. This is where Romy had stayed, and Megan was hoping Romy would be the first of many exciting guests. Megan's mind was already filled with extravagant visions of famous authors coming to share intimate insights into their lives and work; to offer deep discussions of their writing processes and inspirations. Maybe J.K. Rowling would even come, she thought, and maybe J.K. Rowling would sleep in the bedroom down the hall from Megan's own apartment. And maybe, just maybe, they would become best friends, texting each other all day long with tidbits of gossip about the literary world. Not likely, but maybe. Everything was possible.

When the home had been converted, an exterior entrance had been added around the back to get residents to their upstairs rooms without having to go through the library. However, the grand staircase that led from the main floor to the second floor was so grand that everyone had agreed it must stay. It was one of Megan's favorite features, and she now walked down these stairs to the library, her hand caressing the finely sanded yet rustic railing. The main floor had been designed with luxurious fourteen-foot ceilings, giving significant extra height to the staircase. Walking down these stairs always made Megan feel like she was descending into the middle of an exciting adventure. When she wanted to go outside and down to the river, as she did now, it was easier and quicker to use the living quarters entrance. But the allure of the staircase was too great. Megan floated down to the main floor, then headed out the back door.

Morning dew still clung to the grass, so Megan kept to the gravel path that led from the library down to the riverside reading area. She sat at her favorite of the benches and watched the river flow by.

"Susurration," she whispered, remembering Romy's description. She smiled. A new friend, maybe? Not J.K. Rowling, but perhaps just as good. Megan was hesitant to assume that an author as famous as Romy would consider her a friend. Still, they'd gotten on well. Maybe later in the week, Megan thought, she'd give Romy a call, see if she wanted to go out for drinks. With her and Lily, maybe. Who, after all, would turn down the chance of a new friend?

The library sat on a vast expanse of a slower part of the river, but even so, due to recent rains, the water was raging. A large boulder slightly upstream of the seating area broke the surface of the water, even when the river ran as high as it was now. The water swirled and eddied around the boulder, racing around the rock to unite again downstream. Twigs floating downstream had a choice to make: left or right? Most broke around to the left, but on occasion a rogue leaf might break to the right. Megan imagined she could watch the drama of nature for hours. She'd brought a book with her, but nonetheless found herself looking up from the pages for many long minutes at a time, mesmerized as the water coursed by.

She was still sitting there almost an hour later, absorbed in meditation on the water's flow, when she heard someone walking down the path toward her, heels crunching on the gravel. Megan checked her watch: almost nine. Probably time to get on with the day, anyway.

"Hello," called out Max. Megan heard his voice and imagined his smile, but when she turned, she found his look to be quite somber.

"Hey," said Megan, frowning. She wasn't used to seeing Max so serious. "What's up?"

Max walked over to the bench where she sat. He held out his hand toward the seat.

"Yes, of course," said Megan. "Please, have a seat." This clearly was not a social call. Something was disturbing him. Her heart started beating faster as she thought of all the reasons a policeman might come visit her at nine in the morning. Were her parents okay? Lily Bell? Rae? "What's up, Max?" she repeated.

Max leaned forward on the seat, elbows on his knees. He watched the water rush by for a few moments, then shook his head. "I hate this part." He paused. "It's Romy. She's dead." He turned to Megan. Resolution and duty filled his eyes, but behind that, she could see sorrow.

"What!" said Megan. This was impossible news. "Are you serious?" When Megan had left the party the previous day, Romy had been surrounded by a field of friends and well-wishers. Deciding not to break into the conversation, Megan had left without saying goodbye to her host and would-be friend. "What happened?" she asked. "I can't … You're … Did she …?" Famous people were not above depression, Megan knew. Had Romy's own life haunted her to the point of despair?

"We don't know." He paused, then looked at Megan, watching her carefully. "Were you here all night?"

The blood rushed from Megan's face and she broke out into an instant sweat. "You think someone killed her?" Megan said in horror. "You're kidding. I'm a suspect? Max? No!" Her mind raced as she tried to think who could bear witness to her actions last night, but she'd been here at the river, or inside upstairs, alone, the whole night. She hadn't talked to Lily, because Lily had been working. She hadn't gone to Rae's. She hadn't gone anywhere. Why hadn't she gone somewhere? If only—

"Not really, no," said Max. "But it would be remiss of me not to ask. You were at the party, right?"

Megan nodded, willing her heartbeat to return to normal.

"Aside from your own …" he paused. "Including your own alibi, I'm wondering if you might have seen anyone, or heard anything, that might be helpful. You don't have to tell me now. Think about whether anything seemed off, or if anyone was acting strange. Anything at all."

"I hardly knew anyone at the party," Megan said. "But I'll try. Max, I wasn't … I didn't go there planning an alibi. I don't have an alibi. And … she couldn't have …" She shook her head. The party had been filled with strangers; filled with people with unknown motives and desires and demons. She doubted anything she could remember would help, but she would try. Her mind was porridge. Suddenly nothing made sense. "Max," she said, as the officer stood to leave. "How did she die?"

Max glanced at the river as it raced by on its way toward Puget Sound. "She drowned. Or was drowned. In her pool." He seemed on the verge of saying more, but he held his tongue. He nodded his thanks, and left.

The world spun. Everything seemed off. Megan felt she couldn't believe Max; that suddenly she couldn't believe anything. Romy, dead? She couldn't be. She'd been alive just twelve hours before. How could she be dead now? She'd been, what, fifty? Certainly not more than fifty-five. Vibrant, alive, the world her oyster. Everything ahead of her. She'd faced her demons and come out fighting. She'd made her difficult choices. She'd let go of the past. She was on top of the world. Max must be wrong. Romy was not dead.

Somehow, the landscape around Megan hadn't changed at all, as if it was completely indifferent to the drama of humanity. She looked up at the treetops but this time her gaze was inward. "Gus," Megan said out loud, before even thinking the name. "She put that pool in for Gus." But where was Gus? Surely the ex-husband was always Suspect Number One? Megan paused again, then looked at the river. "Lily," she said, pulling her phone from her pocket. As she started texting, a text from Lily came in.

"Did you hear?" Lily's text read.

"Max just left!" Megan texted back.

"I'm swamped," Lily wrote. "B&B is chaos. Romy's agent. Fans calling. They're on their way."

"Fans?" wrote Megan. "On their way?"

"Word spread fast. Coming to mourn and hold a vigil. Needing a place to stay. Will call you later. Meet tonight?" Lily texted.

"Yes," wrote Megan. "Talk soon." She tucked her phone back into her pocket. Who had told the fans already? Must have been someone on Twitter, she decided. News seemed always to break first on Twitter these days.

* * *

When the library opened at noon, news of Romy's death was on everyone's lips. Megan muddled through her usual work but her mind was back at Romy's party. The pool. Megan couldn't stop thinking about the pool. Her brain kept creating a mental image of Romy in the pool, lifeless, face down, her dusty rose skirt floating around her. Patrons who knew that Romy had stayed with Megan a few days asked if she'd heard anything. Megan told them no. It seemed strange that somehow she was expected to have information on this person she barely knew. Stranger still that her emotions were so strong. "It might have been murder," Megan said to herself. "And even if it wasn't, that's still bad. Of course you're upset." She shook her head. The day was feeling surreal. It was wrong, Megan thought, to hope that the murder was personal, but the idea of a random killer on the loose in town was too frightening to bear. "We have to figure this out," Megan said out loud, just as a patron approached her desk.

"What?" said the man. He was short, maybe mid-forties, balding, with an unusually dramatic mustache. He wore a white t-shirt, charcoal jacket without lapels, a long, thin plaid scarf, and faded jeans. He stared at Megan as though her talking had been a rude interruption. "Is there a problem?" he said.

"I'm—sorry, I was just talking to myself." Megan kicked herself internally. Why did women always apologize to strange men? Why did she feel the need to explain and to appease? But she knew the answer: women appeased strange men, because strange men were the kind who would hurt the women who they felt did them wrong. "Can I help you?" It occurred to her that having a way to buzz downstairs to Owen, an alert of some sort, might not be a bad idea. This guy was just a strange man, probably. But with a murderer on the loose …

"Rosemary Grace Garrison," said the man.

Megan blinked. How had he known what she'd been thinking about? No, she thought, of course. Everyone was thinking the same thing. That alone was no cause for alarm. But whatever conversation this man wanted to have, she wasn't sure she wanted to have it. "Yes?" she said patiently.

"Is it true?" he asked.

Internally, Megan sighed heavily. She sometimes hated that part of the job included being polite. What she wanted to say to this man was, "I don't know who you are or what you want, but a woman has died and it's none of your business." Instead, she swallowed her annoyance and smiled. "Is what true, sir?" she asked, knowing full well that this man had an agenda, and men with agendas rarely moved on easily.

"Is she dead?"

The harshness of the man's words hit Megan in the gut, and she found her composure slipping. "I'm sorry, sir. You'll have to ask the police if you have concerns about Ms. Garrison. I can't help you." She turned to her computer and tried to look busy, hoping the man would go away. He did not. She felt the heat rising under her hair at the back of her neck, but she tried to look unruffled.

"She stole my idea," the man said angrily. "She deserved whatever she got." Megan was shocked, but stayed calm. Library work wasn't what it used to be. In many ways, library work had become social work. People came to the library for help of all kinds. A couple of years before, a nearby library system had held a workshop on how to deal with upset patrons, and Megan had jumped at the chance to attend. Now, she was glad. She dug back in her mind to remember what she'd learned. But the only thing she could remember was: stay calm. "I'm a writer," the man continued, unprompted. "I met her once and told her I'm a writer, and I told her about the book I was writing. Next thing I knew, her book came out and the plot was exactly the same as what I'd told her. It was my idea." His voice got louder with every sentence he spoke.

Megan's mind raced. Did she know this man? She couldn't place him, but even in a small town she didn't know everyone. Plus, there were small towns all around the area. He could be from any one of them. How could he have met Romy? Maybe in Seattle? Had he been at the party? She tried to remember but couldn't. "That sounds very frustrating. I'm sorry, sir, what's your name again?" she asked, keeping her voice steady.

The corner of his lip turned up, but the smile went no further than that. "I didn't say, Megan," he said, pointedly reading her nametag. Megan felt at a disadvantage and cringed. "Kirk," he said finally. "Kirk Foster. It should be my book on these shelves, not hers." He stared at Megan as though he expected her to have a solution. "She stole my idea," he said again.

Without even looking, Megan could feel the eyes of other patrons watching them. There was a subdued quiet to the room, more than usual in the library. People were listening. "I can hear that you're upset, Mr. Foster. Unfortunately, there's nothing I can do." She turned to her computer again, thinking right now would be a good time for a refresher course on handling upset patrons. "I can't help" was undoubtedly the wrong thing to say. Should she recommend a psychiatrist to him? Or would that just make it worse? Probably the latter, she thought.

"You women," he said. "Worthless."

Worthless? Something in Megan snapped. *Romy's been murdered. Who is this man? What right does he have to come charging here and ...* She'd only known Romy briefly, but she'd felt connected to her. Sure, maybe that sounded corny, she thought, but who was this man to be so cavalier about everything right after Romy had died? Or, she suddenly thought, did he know something? Did he know more than he was letting on? Didn't murderers often return to the scene of the crime, eager to see the reaction they'd caused? "Sir," she said, "I'm so sorry to hear you had a bad experience." *Get as much out of him as you can,* she thought. *This is the kind of guy who will talk.* "When did you meet her? How did she happen to hear about your idea?"

The man's face turned smug, pleased to think finally someone believed him. "I live over in Sedro-Woolley," he said. "She came to my office when she was looking for someone to build her house. Couple of years ago. I'm in construction, see," he said.

"I thought you were a writer?" Megan said.

"I am," the man said, scowling. "At nights. Construction during the day. She wanted a bid on her house. She came to us and I told her I was a writer, too. We had something in common. Thought I'd butter her up, build a rapport. Told her about my idea. She thought it was amazing. Then she picked another company to do her house and she stole my idea."

The timeline seemed short, Megan thought, but then, Romy had been a fast writer. She'd published two or three books per year, every year, at least. It was possible. Megan wished she could take a photo of the man without him seeing, but instead she focused on remembering what he looked like. Would someone murder over a stolen idea? Or a lost building bid? Or both? But Megan was at a loss of what to do next. She had neither reason nor authority to detain the man. The best she could do would be to pass the information on to Max. "I'm sorry I can't help you, Mr. Foster." She repeated his name in hopes it would help her remember it long enough to write it down after he left.

He grunted and shook his head, as though it was all her fault. Probably, to this sort of man, everything was everyone else's fault; he was the sole innocent victim of the world. He walked away, shaking his head and muttering angrily under his breath as patrons around him exchanged glances and averted their eyes. Megan shuddered as she watched him leave. Did any of his story have merit? Did it matter? How could she find out?

A young girl walked past Megan's desk, a stack of books in her arms, their bright yellow spines standing out against the girl's bright pink jacket. "The girl detective," Megan said to herself, the books' iconic covers instantly recognizable. "What would Nancy Drew do?"

five

Later that afternoon, another familiar face walked in the library's main doors, strolling in with a confidence of a man who owned the place. Of course, he once had. Edison had changed his clothes since the party the day before, but he looked so bedraggled he may as well not have.

Megan saw him before he saw her, his eyes to the rafters, looking around the building like he was seeing ghosts. He seemed haunted, and Megan wondered whether it was recent events or the more distant past that was causing the haggard look on his face. When he saw her, he walked swiftly over.

"Megan," he said. "Terrible news. Just …" He closed his eyes and clenched his jaw. Shook his head and composed himself. "I'm here on library business. Sort of. Romy's …" He shook his head again. "Romy's sister and brother-in-law were staying with her. They can't bear to stay in the house but they don't want to leave town just yet. Can you … can they stay here?"

"Of course, of course," said Megan, wanting to reach out for his hand. "As long as they need. We close in an hour. Tell them to come around to the back door and I'll let them in."

Edison tapped his fingers twice on Megan's desk, his mind a million miles away, and left.

A few minutes later, Megan's cell rang. Caller ID identified the call: Lily. "Hey, what's up?" Megan said on answering.

"Things are crazy here," said Lily, sounding unusually frazzled. Normally she was the calm in the storm, the friend everyone could rely on in any emergency. "There is no room at the inn. Literally. The word is out about Romy and fans are heading to town, and they all want a room. Rae says people have asked to park camper vans in her parking lot, and set up tents on the lawn out back of the pub. It's insane."

"It's crazy all over," said Megan. "I'll have to tell you about this guy who came by here earlier. Creepy. He said Romy had stolen his idea for a book."

"What?" said Lily. "Ah crap, another call coming in. Quick question: Can I send Romy's agent and her husband to stay in one of your guest rooms? With fans staying here it could get weird. I don't want them to feel uncomfortable."

"Of course," said Megan, though she hoped this would be the last such request. There were three guest suites upstairs; with Romy's sister and brother-in-law in one, and now the agent in another, things were starting to get crowded. "Plenty of room. Whatever I can do to help."

"Okay, I'll send them over now. I don't think I can come see you tonight. I'll call as soon as I can. Gotta go. Love you!"

"Love you, too! Hang in there!" said Megan, but Lily had already moved on to her other call.

"Well then," Megan said to her desk, "someone had better make sure all those guest rooms are set up for guests." After notifying an assistant, she headed up the grand staircase to get ready for company.

* * *

It felt wrong to have people stay in the suite Romy had been in so recently, so Megan prepared the other two suites instead and then went back to her own apartment. Guessing that the arriving company wouldn't want to go out to dinner that night, she rummaged through her cupboards to see if she could provide some sort of a meal. When she'd accepted the offer to live over the library she hadn't expected so many B&B duties, but it seemed a small price to pay for what she was getting in return.

However, "go to the grocery store" had been on Megan's to-do list for more than a week. The cupboards were nearly bare. "It'll have to be spaghetti," she said to the kitchen, grabbing pasta and sauce from the pantry shelves. "Maybe I have the makings for meatballs?" she speculated. On rummaging around some more she decided she did, if she improvised a bit.

Emlyn and Baz, Romy's agent and her husband, arrived first, shortly after five. Half an hour later, Romy's sister, Sylvie, and Sylvie's husband, Wade, showed up. Megan got everyone settled into their rooms. When she saw Emlyn's pristine Louis Vuitton suitcase, she had second thoughts about whether her spaghetti dinner would be good enough, but Emlyn seemed distracted and happy to be served. Megan showed them the way to her own apartment, and told them to come over whenever they liked.

As Megan was laying the table, the outside doorbell rang once again. "But everyone's here," said Megan to the kitchen as she answered her phone to buzz the visitor in. "Hello?" she said, her voice raising an extra level at the end in question.

"Megan? It's Edison. Thought I'd come over and help with the guests if you need help. Should I come up?" Edison said, sounding more uncertain than Megan had ever heard him.

"Of course. We're having dinner here in a bit. You should join us. Come on up." She buzzed him in. A few minutes later he was up the elevator from the downstairs back lobby, and at her door.

"I brought wine," Edison said by way of greeting, lifting the bag he was holding. He had indeed brought wine: six bottles.

"That should be enough," Megan said with a grin. "So thoughtful. Thank you. Please, come in." She suddenly felt so awkward. Hosting a dinner party for people she didn't know, all of whom were mourning someone she'd only just met. What kind of small talk could she hope to make that would be in any way appropriate? She should have left them alone. They would have found food on their own. Instead she was forcing everyone together for an uncomfortable dinner. Her intentions had been good, but the execution left something to be desired.

"They're all coming here for dinner," Megan blurted out. "I'm not sure this was a good idea. I wasn't thinking." The look in her eyes was one of panic.

Edison put the wine down. "Hey, hey, hey," he said, pulling her in for an unexpected hug. Ordinarily Megan might have stiffened at the familiarity, but she collapsed into his warmth. It seemed they both needed the comfort. After a few moments, Edison pulled away, held her at arms' length, and looked in her eyes. "There's no right or wrong here. There's just people do- ing their best. When I called to check that everything was okay, Sylvie told me you'd invited them to dinner. I could hear in her voice how grateful she was. You've done good. And I'm here to offer support, to you or to whoever needs it."

Tears started to rise in Megan's eyes and she blinked them away. "Thank you, Edison," she said with a heavy sigh. "And the same goes for you. You knew Romy well?" she said, her voice making the statement into a question.

Edison dropped his hands and picked up the wine, turning away from Megan and heading to the kitchen. "Do you have a bottle opener?" he said.

Out of bounds, Megan thought, and she let the subject go.

She thought back on her previous interactions with Edison. She'd been living in Emerson Falls for about a dozen years now, and she knew that Edison—and, until the divorce about three years ago, his wife—had been living in the area on and off for years, a few weeks at a time. After the divorce, Edison had moved to the area permanently. He'd earned his millions long ago, back in his twenties, in software. More recently he'd created a game app that had brought him another influx of income. It was after that that he'd decided his wife should become his ex-wife. She hadn't taken to the idea all that well, especially considering the prenup she'd signed when they got married which left her with almost nothing. The divorce had provided the town with triple scoops of gossip on a near-daily basis for a good while.

But while divorces could bring out the worst in people, that didn't mean those people were inherently awful. She remembered Romy's thoughts on the man: charming, but dangerous. Megan agreed with the former, but was less convinced on the latter. Electric, certainly; before he'd moved to town full time, she'd always felt she could tell when he was in the area. It was like he carried with him a charge that energized everything anywhere near him. He was a man of ideas, and those ideas seemed to be generated from physical activity. He never sat still. Every morning, and sometimes again in the evening, he could be found running down the highway that ran past town. Even while sitting in a meeting he'd have a toe tapping in time to his unspoken thoughts, as ideas formed and internal brainstorms brewed. In library planning meetings he would jump out of his chair when he had a sudden idea, or when anyone said anything that excited him. It was hard not to feel a sense of excitement around him, an eagerness, a burgeoning of possibilities.

Megan liked him.

As Edison opened a bottle of red, there was another knock at the door. Megan let in Emlyn and Baz, and then just as she was about to close the door saw Sylvie and Wade heading down the hallway. She waited with the door open, and let them in as well.

Sylvie's eyes were red and puffy. Megan looked her over and could see the resemblance to Romy. Sylvie was three years older, Megan had read, and was slightly taller, but sported a similar bob haircut on her pure white hair. *Just as I suspected*, Megan thought, recalling that she'd imagined this is how Romy's hair would look as she aged. *But she'll never age now.* Where Romy had been bubbly, Sylvie seemed introspective. It was impossible to know at this point whether that was her normal demeanor, or a reaction to the tragedy. Sylvie's husband, Wade, was an inch or so taller than Sylvie. He had a thick head of graying hair, and bright blue-gray eyes that were somewhat aloof or distracted as he greeted Megan and thanked her for her kindness. "We appreciate the hospitality," Wade said. "Romy had told us how gracious you were, letting her stay here. We just couldn't be at her house right now." As he said it, he reached his arm protectively around Sylvie's waist.

"Of course, anything," said Megan. "Whatever you need, please, let me know. Anything." She mentally halted her babbling and showed them the way to the living room.

Edison was already serving the wine, and Emlyn and Baz were seated on the couch. The living room was not tiny, but neither was it huge. Megan was just glad she had enough chairs and couches for everyone. The weight of Romy's death—murder—filled the room and started to stifle Megan. Recognizing that this was a meal for sustenance, not socializing, Megan excused herself once everyone was settled. "Dinner's almost ready," she said, and headed to the kitchen.

The murmur of voices from the living room was muted and interspersed with long silences as Megan finished preparing the meal. She quickly brought the dishes out to the dining room.

"We're ready," she said, and the group found places at the table. As the host of the meal, Megan felt like she should be leading the conversation, but she was at a loss and the evening was quiet and strained. Finally, Wade broke the silence. "Megan, this is an unusual situation you have here. Is it common for a librarian to live over the library?"

Small talk, to be sure, but Megan was glad for something to cling to. "No, actually." She nodded her head at Edison. "This used to be Edison's vacation home. He donated it to the county to be used as a library, but it's so enormous that they decided to make the top floor into living space for the Library Director and guests."

This sparked Wade's interest. He turned to Edison. "A spectacular home. What made you decide to give it up?" he asked.

Edison smiled, his tired eyes brightening just the slightest. "I've never been one for ostentatiousness. If it had been up to me, this house would have been a tenth of this size, at most. It's ridiculous. It shouldn't take several minutes to get from one end of a house to the other. You feel like you need a search party sometimes to find the other person. My ex-wife, Daphne, wanted this house. 'I've always wanted a big vacation home, Ed,' she said." His upper lip curled slightly at the memory. "I hate being called Ed, and she knew it, but she did it because it amused her to irritate me. 'Make me a big vacation home, Ed.' The marriage was already on rocky ground, and I wanted to try to … make her happy, so I said yes. I had no interest in it, and at the time I was busy with work, so she was in charge of the whole thing. Next thing I know, she comes to me with the blueprints for this." He looked around the room, seeing beyond the walls. "I was too exhausted to argue, and at that point I still thought there might be something I could do to … to save us." He twirled some spaghetti around on his fork, watching the pale strands loop over themselves and make tiny splatters of sauce. "I never could make her happy. I'm not sure she ever wanted to actually be happy. Looking back, I think all she wanted was for everyone around her to keep trying to make her happy. She didn't love people. She didn't love me. She loved attention. She loved the attention I showered on her, doing everything I could to convince her to finally love me back. That was her idea of love." He paused to take a bite of his food, and sat staring at his fork a while before he continued. "Finally I'd had enough. Filed for divorce. Luckily for me, my dad had been very insistent that I have Daphne sign a prenup," a small, satisfied smile turned up the corners of his lips. "She got next to nothing. Knowing how much the county could use a nice new library, I thought the best thing I could do would be to sign this building over." His smile grew. "Daphne hated reading."

Wade shook his head in mild admiration at Edison's audacity. "Was she angry?"

A burst of caustic laughter erupted from Edison. "Was she angry!" He reached for the wine and refilled his glass, then held up the bottle to see if anyone else wanted more. Megan nodded, and he passed the wine down to her. "Like I said, however she may have looked on the outside, Daphne was never happy. I don't know if it bothered her more that I gave away the house or that I stopped trying to make her happy."

"Does she still live around here?" Wade asked.

Edison shuddered. "Can't get rid of her," he said. "She doesn't live here in Emerson Falls, but she's a few towns over. Always watching," he said. "Never gave much attention to me when we were married, but now that I'm gone, she won't go away. Anything I do, I hear about three days later. When I trace the source, it always comes back to her. No idea how she finds out, but she does."

"How long ago was the divorce?" asked Baz, doing his part to keep the conversation going. Sylvie was silent and listless, seemingly unaware of the conversation going on around her. Wade's attention seemed to be more centered on his wife. Emlyn was listening, but she seemed unfocused as well.

"Two years," said Edison. "I'm a new man. Life's never been better." He winked at Megan. Her heart fluttered, not from attraction but from uncertainty: why was he winking at her?

"Did your ex-remarry?" asked Baz. A sidelong glance at his wife made Megan wonder if Baz found the idea of being a free man again appealing.

"No," Edison said, wiping the corners of his mouth with his napkin. "Not yet. I don't think she's even dated. Apparently the rest of the men in the world are smarter than I was." He put his napkin down. "But, not my concern."

By this time, everyone had stopped eating. Megan stood to gather plates. "I don't have much for dessert," she said. "Sorry, I didn't have time to get to the store. I think there's some ice cream if anyone wants some?"

Wade looked over at his wife. Clearly her attention was not in the room. "I think we're good," he said. "All we needed was a little something to keep us going. You were good to invite us, but I think we'll head back to our rooms and rest."

"Of course, yes," said Megan. She quickly whisked the dishes to the kitchen, noticing Sylvie had hardly eaten. When she returned, Wade and Sylvie had made their way to the front door.

"Before you go back to your room—" Megan said, and then she opened the door that led from her apartment to the hallway that led to the other rooms. She looked at Sylvie. "May I show you something?"

For the first time in an hour it seemed Sylvie was back in the present. "Yes?" she said.

Megan led Sylvie and Wade down the hallway to the door that separated the library from the living quarters. Opening the door, she took them down the grand staircase, into the library, and over to a wide open space that had once been part of the home's "great room." The room jutted out beyond the rest of the building toward the river, its corners cut so the space had the shape of half of an octagon. Large, strong panes of glass filled the walls from eighteen inches off the ground all the way up to nearly the top of the high ceiling. Thick rustic columns between the panes gave support to the building, and framed the view out over the water and the sky and the trees. In the home's new life as a library, the space was now set up as a reading area, with cozy, overstuffed leather chairs and ottomans, low tables with reading lamps, and a gas fireplace at one side.

"Sometimes, I like to come sit down here, by myself, when the library is closed," Megan said quietly. "Even though I have a really nice apartment upstairs, there's just something comforting about being in the library. All of humanity is here," she said, looking around at the stacks of books. "Every pain a person has ever endured, every joy, everything anyone has ever felt, it's in here. When I'm here with all these thoughts, I never feel alone. When I'm here, I always know that others have gone through worse, and survived." She looked at Sylvie. "I don't know if it would help you. But you're free to use it, if you need to come and sit and think, and be alone without being alone. The library opens at noon, and staff start coming around eleven-thirty. But other than that, consider all this yours."

Sylvie looked around the nook, her eyes glistening in the dim light. "Thanks," she said softly. "I just might."

Megan showed Sylvie and Wade how to turn on the fireplace and where the light switches were, and then they all headed back upstairs.

Sylvie and Wade said goodnight and disappeared into their suite. Megan realized she'd left the others without a thought. When she walked back into her apartment, though, she found the weight of the room had lifted a bit, and the buzz of the conversation was lighter again as well.

"How long have you been a literary agent?" Edison was saying as Megan made her way back into the living room. He was seated in one of Megan's favorite chairs, seemingly relaxed with his half-full glass of wine, but still he looked ready to spring out of the chair at any moment. When she looked closely, though, Megan could see his eyes were still tired, still haunted. Megan wondered if he ever really let his guard down, or if always being busy was his way of coping with life.

"Eight years," Emlyn said. "Just a few months with Romy. Her regular agent just had a baby a month ago. I guess I'll have to find another superstar to hitch my wagon to now," she said. Emlyn didn't seem to notice the puzzled look that crossed Edison's face, but Megan did.

"And you?" Baz asked Edison. "How did you know Romy?" He was leaning forward, elbows on knees, his eyes slightly glazed over. Megan wondered if he'd started drinking in their room before coming to dinner. "A hot property like her, that would have appealed to me, too, if I'd been on the prowl." Emlyn swatted at his arm without looking at him.

"She wasn't anyone's property," Megan mumbled. She regretted her outburst, but no one seemed to have heard.

"We met at some author thing she did a while back," Edison said vaguely. "Before I was divorced even. I'm a big reader. That's why I wanted this house to become a library. I'd read most if not all of her books at the time. I went to the event, and struck up a conversation with her, and we hit it off."

It occurred to Megan that once a person was gone, their side of the story was gone with them. Had Edison and Romy hit it off right away? From what Romy had told her, she wouldn't have described it that way. But it could still be true. Romy may have downplayed the meeting, or Edison could be exaggerating, or the truth could lie somewhere in between. Megan remembered thinking at the party, when Edison wrapped his arm around Romy's waist, that the relationship seemed deeper than Romy had indicated. If, in fact, Romy had been intentionally misleading about how close she was to the man, why had she done so? From whom was she trying to hide it? Herself? Someone else? On the other hand, hadn't Megan herself fallen into Edison's arms when he had arrived just an hour earlier? And if he wrapped his arm around her just now, might she not reciprocate? Maybe he was just a man who inspired close touch. On this, the jury was out.

"And you were dating?" Emlyn probed. "You and Romy?"

Was that a hint of a blush on Edison's cheeks? "No, no, not at all," said Edison. He smiled. "She wouldn't have me."

So at least that much was true, thought Megan.

"Not yet, anyway," continued Edison. "I can be quite convincing." He looked at Megan. She could feel him flirting, but she could also feel the strain he seemed to be under. He hadn't had time to even begin to process Romy's death yet. Maybe that's why he had come over, she thought. Maybe he wasn't ready to think about what had happened just yet.

"I'll bet," said Emlyn, with a flirtatious smile. Baz seemed unconcerned and unimpressed. "Say, you're a big man in town," continued Emlyn, seemingly oblivious to whatever Edison might be feeling. "What have the police told you about the murder? They won't tell us anything, and my bosses want to know what to tell the fans."

"Oh, the fans," said Megan, out loud, unintentionally. The others turned to her in curiosity.

"Yes?" said Emlyn. "What about them?"

"Just that they're on their way. Lily—my friend who runs the B&B—she said they're coming to town, some sort of vigil."

"Oh, that's right," said Emlyn evenly. "That's why she kicked us out."

Megan bristled. Lily had sent the agent and her husband over to the library out of concern for them and their mental well-being. "She wanted to make sure you weren't disturbed in this difficult time," she said, mustering up as much warmth and sincerity as she could.

"Well, it's nice enough here in Edison's old home," Emlyn said, bursting into a special smile again just for the rich bachelor in her midst. It occurred to Megan that perhaps Emlyn was a gold digger; that Romy had told her about Edison and Emlyn had decided to chase him down herself. Baz was such a wet blanket that he hardly seemed to notice anything. Emlyn could flirt with someone right in front of him—as she was—and he'd never know or care.

"They haven't told me anything," said Edison. "All I know is that she drowned." Edison looked at Megan to see if she knew more. Megan shook her head.

"Well," said Emlyn, "my bet is it was that ex-husband of hers. It's always the ex-husband, isn't it?"

"Was he at the party?" said Megan. She hadn't seen him, but then, she'd left early.

"Who else would it be?" said Emlyn. "No one else had a motive. Everyone loved Romy."

Something about the way Emlyn said it made Megan look her over again. Was there jealousy in that tone? "You're from New York, right?" said Megan. "What a long trip to make for a housewarming." She left the unanswered question hanging.

"Originally Pennsylvania, but yes, I'm in New York now. And no, it's not a long trip at all," said Emlyn. "I fly all over the country all the time to work with authors. First class isn't too bad, usually. Romy told me about the housewarming and I thought it would be fun to see a quaint little logging town."

Quaint little logging town? Megan internally rolled her eyes, but outwardly smiled. *Remember, you're the host*, she told herself.

"It was so nice you could come. I'm sure Romy appreciated it."

Edison drained the last dregs of wine from his glass and stood. "I'm sorry to leave you all here," he said, "but it's been a long day. Megan, thanks again for dinner and for hosting our guests." He turned to Emlyn and Baz. "If you need anything, you have my number. I know I'm leaving you in very good hands." He turned to Megan and gave her a long look full of meaning. Exactly what that meaning was, Megan wasn't sure, but the look was full. "Thank you," he said, finally. He grabbed his coat out of the hall closet, and left.

"Well, I guess we'd better be going, too," said Emlyn, yawning. Megan clearly was not as thrilling company to her as Edison had been.

"If you need anything, you know where to find me," Megan said, as Emlyn and Baz walked out the door.

As she watched them walk down he hall, Megan saw Emlyn lean over to Baz, whisper something, and look back over her shoulder at Megan. Seeing Megan standing there watching, Emlyn elbowed Baz, and laughed.

six

The next morning, Megan wondered whether she should make breakfast for her guests. Something told her Sylvie and Wade wouldn't expect it, but Emlyn and Baz might. "Well, then, I won't," she said decisively as she sat on the balcony in her fluffy bathrobe and slippers. Her peppermint tea in her favorite yellow mug warmed her hands. The river was still running high, but the day was clear. As far as she could see, there were no eagles around. "I'm definitely going to need a telescope," she said to the trees, "when winter comes." But for now, the birds were absent.

"Susurration," Megan said, the word popping into her head out of nowhere. The constant hum of the river was so familiar to her by now that she almost didn't notice it anymore.

Megan reached for her phone on the table next to her and checked the time: just after seven-thirty. She opened up her messages and sent a quick text to Lily. "Meet at Rae's at 10." Rae technically didn't open the pub until eleven, but Megan knew she'd be there, and that she'd let them in.

After a few minutes, Lily wrote back. "Okay. Why?"

"We are detectives. We are solving a mystery." Megan wrote.

"Of course we are," wrote Lily.

"I'll invite Max, too," wrote Megan. "And Kevin. He might have seen something."

"Good idea," wrote Lily. "How are your guests?"

"You sent me the agent just to get rid of her, didn't you?" Megan wrote.

Lily's response was a series of laughing emojis.

* * *

After checking with her guests to make sure they had what they needed, including keys to get into the living quarters and their rooms, Megan headed over to Rae's. Rae had confirmed that they would be welcome to use her space as Crime Solving Headquarters. Both Max and Kevin said they'd be there, too.

When Megan arrived, Rae was in the kitchen prepping food for the day. Max was also in the pub, sitting at a thick wooden table rather than the bar, reading something on his tablet. "What's on the menu today?" Megan called out to Rae as she pulled out a chair at Max's side.

"You'll eat it and you'll like it!" was Rae's only response.

"Good old Rae," laughed Max, his eyes and teeth twinkling as he looked up to greet Megan. "So you're a detective now?" he said. "I can always use extra minds. This one is tricky."

"They're doing an autopsy, I assume?" said Megan. A pitcher of water and four glasses had been set out. Megan poured herself a glass and took a sip.

"Yes, all that. Autopsy, toxicology. Preliminary results are in: drowning. Drownings are tough. It's almost impossible to tell whether a drowning is a homicide. But an accidental drowning seems unlikely, and suicidal drowning is really difficult. The body fights it too hard." He sighed and shook his head.

"Plus, she didn't seem suicidal," said Megan.

Max shrugged. "I didn't know her well enough to say. People commit suicide all the time and their friends and family had no idea they were having troubles. We'll need to talk to more people about her state of mind. But certainly there were no obvious indicators. Regardless, all signs point to homicide."

"Romy's sister and brother-in-law and her agent and the agent's husband are staying in the library guest rooms for now. I had them over for dinner last night. Edison Finley Wright came over too. We talked a bit, but it was pretty subdued. I didn't feel like I got a lot of insight into anything. Emlyn thought Romy's ex-husband, Gus, was the obvious culprit."

Max nodded. "Yeah, we're definitely looking into Gus." He paused. "By the way, you know this is a sensitive situation. I could use any help you can offer, but of course we need discretion."

Megan rolled her eyes. "Max. I'm a librarian," she said.

He raised an eyebrow. "Meaning …?"

"Meaning, librarians have to be discreet. We can see everyone's entire checkout history. Whether you're in the 294.3 section, or the 613.9 section, I say nothing," Megan said.

"And what, exactly, are at 294.3 and 613.9?" Max twinkled.

"You will just have to come to my house and find out," Megan said with a coy smile.

The outside door burst open, framing Lily as she held the door for Kevin, who was running up close behind her. "You rang?" Lily said, shrugging off her jacket and then re-adjusting her ponytail before sitting next to Megan. Kevin took the remaining seat. He nodded at Megan with a small, enigmatic smile that made her again regret not having kept in touch with him.

"Yes," said Megan. "Max is here, obviously, to remind us to be professionals. But I think we, with all our brilliant minds, could be of great help to him, by sharing what we may have seen or heard the night of the party. Or any other time."

The kitchen doors swung open and Rae appeared, her chin-length white-blonde hair clipped back into a small bun and her white apron clean but for a fresh tomato stain across the front. "New salsa recipe," she said as she brought in a tray of chips and salsa. "Just made it up. Let me know what you think." She put the appetizers down and walked away without waiting for a response.

"Well, where do we start?" Lily said, reaching for a chip. "I was at the party, but to be honest, I was more concerned with making sure the food trays stayed full than I was with watching for murder suspects."

"Same," said Kevin, his eyes on the food. "I wasn't even with the guests. Just outside with the cars."

"Once we get talking I'll bet you'll think of something," Megan said. She'd brought a pen and yellow legal pad with her, and now at the top of the first page she wrote "ROMY" in all capitals, underlining it twice. "Kevin, doesn't your girlfriend—didn't your girlfriend work for Romy?" she asked.

He nodded. "Yeah, personal assistant. Out of a job now, I guess. She's smart." He looked at Max. "Have you talked to her already?"

"Not yet," said Max, typing a note into his tablet. "What's her name?"

"Courtney," Kevin said, bobbing his head ever so slightly. "Courtney Shaw." He ran his hand rapidly back and forth over his short hair, like he was petting a dog that was a very good boy.

"S-h-a-w?" Max asked.

"Yeah, that's it," Kevin said.

Megan wrote this down on her legal pad next to a bullet point. "Courtney Shaw," she said as she wrote. "Kevin's girlfriend."

Kevin looked at the pad of paper and then at Megan, but said nothing.

"How long have you been dating?" Max asked, his tone casual.

Kevin bristled slightly and shifted his chin. The question was normally an innocent one, but somehow in these circumstances everything took on new meaning. "A little over a year," he said. Megan wrote this down.

"And she's been with Romy for ..." Max left the sentence for Kevin to finish.

"A few years?" said Kevin. "I'm not really sure."

"She's not from Emerson Falls, is she?" said Megan. "I don't remember seeing her before Romy got here."

"She lives in Rockport," said Kevin. "Before that, Hawaii. Before that, Austin, Texas. Before that, east coast somewhere. Look, you should ask her these things, not me. I don't want to get something wrong." He shifted in his seat.

"Okay, I'll talk to her. Thanks," Max said. He made some notes on his tablet.

"Rockport, Hawaii, Austin, east coast," Megan said, writing quickly. "I think," she said, hoping to break the tension that had suddenly built up, "that maybe we should just brainstorm. You know how they say there are no bad ideas in brainstorming. Everyone we can think of with a motive. Anyone? The ex-husband is already on the list," she said, and then she added a bullet point under Courtney's and added his name. "Gus. I don't know his last name. Is he also Garrison?"

His mouth full of chips and salsa, Max nodded. After swallowing, he confirmed: "Yes, Gus Garrison. On the list."

"Okay," said Megan, writing "Garrison" next to "Gus," then adding "ex-husband," with an arrow in between. "Who else? I can think of a few people. For one, there's a guy who came by the library yesterday. Kirk Foster. He said he's a writer, and that Romy stole his idea for a book." Another bullet point on her legal pad: "Kirk Foster, author —> plagiarism?"

Max tapped on his tablet, adding Kirk Foster to his list as well. "Did he say anything that made you suspicious?"

"He was just creepy," said Megan. "Gave me the heebie-jee-bies." She shuddered at the memory.

"Heebie-jeebies," said Max. "Noted." He smiled at Megan and typed on his tablet. Megan hoped he was writing "heebie-jeebies."

"What about any boyfriends or anything?" said Lily. "Was she dating anyone?"

Megan hesitated. Of course Edison couldn't be guilty. Certainly not Edison, with his warm hugs and his generous heart. But if they were brainstorming, they had to include everyone until they could be ruled out. "I don't know what was going on between Romy and Edison," she said, trying to keep it light. "They weren't really an item, I don't think, but there might have been some interest there. Oh!" she suddenly had a thought. "Edison's ex-wife. Daphne. I think her last name is still Wright. She sounds like the kind of person who doesn't want someone else to have what she can't have. If Edison and Romy were dating, maybe that bothered her."

"Enough to kill?" said Lily, skeptical. She grabbed a napkin to wipe up a drop of salsa she'd spilled.

"I have no idea. Edison was talking about her last night, and she didn't seem like the most charming woman in the world," Megan said.

"People don't always talk nice about their exes," Kevin offered.

"That is a good point," Megan said, tapping her pen against the legal pad. She added two bullet points to her list: "Edison —> (no)" and "Daphne Wright —> (bitter ex-wife, yuk)." "Well, we can keep her on the list anyway, for now. What about while you were parking cars, Kevin? Anything unusual strike you?"

Kevin shook his head. "I was focused on trying not to drive anyone's car into the mud. Romy's agent, though, she was a number. Didn't tip, for one thing. And she was yelling at her husband the whole time, up until another guest came near. Then she suddenly flipped, all smiles and saccharin. People like that, who talk in front of 'the help' like we're not even there, can't stand 'em." He rubbed his head again.

Megan thought back to the night before, and her own decision this morning not to feed her guests. Emlyn hadn't particularly impressed her, either. "They're all staying upstairs at the library, you know. Emlyn and Baz, and also Romy's sister and her husband. I have to admit, my subconscious must not like Emlyn as much either. I put her and Baz in the room that has the worst view. But it's not like it's a bad room. Anyway, I fed them last night because I didn't think they'd want to go out, so they all came over to my apartment. She was really flirty with Edison," Megan said, leaning back and stretching her arms over her head. "Emlyn was. Right in front of Baz. I mean, that means nothing. Like you said, just because someone is a jerk doesn't make them a murderer. But for our investigative purposes, let's say it could. Would it be enough motive that she saw Edison as a catch, a millionaire she could ensnare in her web, maybe divorce Baz, marry up? But Romy was in the way? Emlyn would have seen how Edison and Romy interacted. If she had her eye on the prize, she might have wanted to get the competition out of the way. She seems heartless enough." On her legal pad, she wrote "Emlyn —> (gold digger?)" and underlined the name.

Lily laughed. "I get the feeling you aren't adding Emlyn to your Christmas card list," she said.

Megan rolled her eyes and smiled. "Not just yet," she said.

"Hmmm," said Max, unconvinced. "Well, I'll put her down." Once again he tapped away on his tablet.

"What about the sister and brother-in-law?" said Lily. "Why were they here? That seems like a long way to come just for a housewarming party."

"But they're sisters," said Megan. "Of course she'd come visit."

"Max, do you know who the beneficiaries of Romy's will were?" Lily asked.

Max looked from Lily to Megan. "The sister," he said. "Exclusively."

"Not the husband?" said Lily. Max shook his head.

"It can't be Sylvie," Megan objected. "She's too sweet. And her husband is … well, he's polite, anyway." Maybe Wade had been a little aloof, she thought, but he was kind enough.

"They're staying with you, though, so maybe you can find out more," said Lily. "Can't hurt to talk to them and get a feel for their relationship with Romy. Maybe they secretly hated each other."

"And—discreetly—" Max shot Megan a gentle warning look, "find out more about Romy. Who she was," he said. "Find out if they knew whether she'd made anyone angry."

"Or had any crazed fans," said Lily.

Rae walked in and pulled up a chair, handing Kevin a beer and taking a sip from a bottle she'd brought out for herself. "Some of those fans are already in town," she said, dipping a chip into the salsa. "I heard they're having a vigil out at Emerson Falls Park this afternoon."

"How did you hear that?" said Megan, amazed at the way information seemed to float through the air into Rae's ears. "You're not even open yet!"

"I hear things," Rae said, shrugging, a satisfied smile on her face.

"A vigil?" said Max. "Anything official, or they're just gathering there?"

"Just a gathering," Rae said. She ate her chip and salsa. "Mmmmm. Dang, you people. I'm too good to you. This is delicious."

Max dipped a chip into the salsa. "Could use more cilantro,

though," he said. He looked at the assembled motley crew. "Could any of you make it to the vigil this afternoon? See if you can talk to the fans, keep your ears open, see if they have any theories or information? I'll go, too, but I don't know how much they'd say to me in my uniform. Sometimes that turns people off. Maybe you can strike up some conversations."

"Undercover civilian work," said Megan with mock earnestness. "We're on it, Cap'n. I'll see if the staff can cover the library for a couple of hours for me, but I'm sure they can. Lily, are you in?"

"Unfortunately not," Lily said. "Those very fans are taking over the B&B, and I promised Steve I'd be there to help watch over everything. He's been doing so much of the work lately. I can't abandon him again."

Megan turned to Kevin. "How about you? Are you off work this afternoon?" She realized she wasn't entirely sure what Kevin was doing for work these days, but she guessed it was an assortment of odd jobs.

Kevin lifted his shoulders. "I could go for a bit, sure."

"What time are they all gathering at the park, O Oracle?" Megan said, looking at Rae. "I'm assuming you know, since you seem to know everything." She leaned back in her chair and looked out the window. It was getting near opening time, and the locals would be swarming the pub soon.

Rae winked and took drink of her beer. "About one," she said. "They're stopping here for burgers first. Someone tipped them off about Rae's Famous Burgers. Which reminds me," she said, getting up, "I need to get cooking."

Max checked the time. "Quarter to eleven now," he said. "Okay, I'll plan to be at the park around one. Megan and Kevin, if you hear anything, let me know. Or Lily, someone at the B&B might say something interesting. Keep your ears to the ground."

Lily mocked putting her ear to the ground. "Yes, sir." She

stood. "I've got to get back to the inn. Megan, I'll try to come by soon. We're due for a night out, once Deputy Max figures this all out." She gave warm hugs all around and left.

Kevin gulped the last of his beer and stood. "I'm out, too. See you at the vigil," he said to Megan. He gave Max a quick salute, and followed Lily out the door.

Megan stayed in her seat, her mind tumbling. Max watched her, knowing she had a thought brewing, but waiting for it to finish cooking. Finally, Megan looked at him. "Max," she said.

"Yes, Megan?" he said with a smile.

"There are four people in my house, all of whom are, potentially, murder suspects." Her mind was so focused on the mystery at hand that she didn't even notice she was finally referring to the space as "my house." "Do you think I should be worried? None of them is actually guilty, right? They can't be. Emlyn is the most likely of all of them, but I can't imagine her drowning someone." She pursed her lips. Could Emlyn drown someone? Maybe? This idea did not sit well. Having guests was one thing. Harboring a murderer? Well, that was not in the job description.

"Not even with her husband's help?" said Max, his eyebrows raised.

Megan gasped. "So you think they *did* do it? Do you?" A chill ran through Megan's blood. The locks on the doors to her apartment, they were all new and fresh … they should hold …

"I'm not saying that," said Max. "What I'm saying is, I can't rule anyone out yet. Emlyn and Baz are each other's alibis, and that's not particularly convincing."

"I don't have an alibi, either," said Megan pointedly.

Max paused, then looked down at his tablet, and back at Megan. "And I haven't ruled you out, yet, either," he said.

Megan's mouth fell open, but she had no words. It was time to solve this murder.

seven

By noon, the sun's rays had burst through the clouds and the day had turned unseasonably warm, so Megan decided to walk the mile and a half from the library to the park. In Megan's opinion, Emerson Falls, the waterfalls from which the town and the park derived their names, was one of the world's best hidden secrets. Emerson Falls, the town, was tucked into a loop of land that extended out between Highway 20—the North Cascades Highway—on the north, and the Skagit River on the south. Unlike many of the small towns in the area, most of tiny Emerson Falls was not located directly on the highway; people were more likely to go to Emerson Falls by intention than by mistake. As such, very few people accidentally tumbled upon Emerson Falls, the waterfalls. Instead, cars raced by on the highway, never realizing that this masterpiece of nature was less than half a mile away. But Megan knew, and she was excited to have a reason to visit. "I need to come out here more often," she said to herself as she walked toward the park.

The library was situated in the southwestern corner of the

town, in an expanse of land that jutted out into a curve of the river. The falls themselves were on the eastern side of the town, a bit inland from the river that their waters emptied into. As she strolled east along the riverside trail, Megan breathed deeply. The trail itself had been graveled over in the past, but native and non-native plants were poking their green tips through the rocks and growing along the edges in their indomitable quest for life. She spotted the ever-present and invasive reed canary grass, and wondered as she often did whether invasive plants would one day take over the world. Alongside the reed canary grass grew rushes and other grasses, and the ubiquitous Oregon grape.

About halfway between the library and the falls, she came upon a small riverside park, a memorial garden planted some hundred years prior in honor of Adeline "Addie" Emerson, first wife of Chester Robert Emerson, for whom Emerson Falls (both waterfalls and town) had been named. As was the way with so many women in her time, Addie had given her husband five children before she was twenty-seven, then met her death while giving birth to the sixth. Chester had declared that the plants within the park should reflect Addie's English–Scottish–Dutch heritage, and to this day, volunteers dutifully maintained the English yew and field roses, the Scottish gorse and heather, and a riot of tulips, all now in glorious bloom. A short white picket fence, recently painted, marked the perimeter of the park. Megan was tempted to slip through the gate and sit a while on the bench with its ancient plaque:

In Memory of
beloved Wife and Mother
Adeline Rose Emerson
Ever in Our Hearts

However, with her goal in mind, she walked on.

A rustling sound in the bushes stopped Megan in her tracks. The rustling stopped, too, and Megan wondered if she'd been mistaken. "Don't be a snake," Megan whispered to whatever had made the noise. She hated snakes, regardless of whether they could hurt her. She froze, and slowed her breathing in an effort to hear better, but for many long seconds there was no movement from anywhere, not even a whisper of the wind. Then, suddenly, in a flurry of movement, a bird burst out of the bush and flew away. Megan put her hand to her heart as it raced in response to the sudden activity. "A hawk?" Megan said, squinting into the sunshine for any identifying features before the bird was out of sight. Medium-sized bird with a large head; long, rounded tail with dark brown stripes and a white tip; dark gray cap; yellow feet. "Cooper's hawk," she decided. "Goodbye, Cooper's hawk," she said to the quickly disappearing creature, and then continued on her journey.

Eventually, she left the riverside trail, crossed the main road in town, and followed the escalating roar of the waterfalls until she reached the park. Although people were already gathering near the gazebos, Megan first headed deeper into the park to pay homage to the waterfalls.

Rivers were loud, Megan thought as she approached, but nothing could match the unrelenting thunder of these falls. And she loved it. Somehow, the roar of these waterfalls could push out thoughts of past and future; the noise filled her ears and her soul and left room for nothing but the present. Megan inhaled deeply, filling her lungs with the scents of the forest: the rich, damp earth; the slight mustiness of the bark of the trees; the cool, mist-thickened air; the freshness of evergreen needles and moss; the mineral smell of the rocks as the water sloughed off infinitesimal grains, smoothing them out over millennia. The falls and the forest always seemed to lecture Megan about patience and time and priorities, about being in this moment even while paying homage to eternity.

Emerson Falls was actually made up of several separate drops and turns, and Megan took the time to follow the winding half-mile nature loop along the water's edge and through the forest of ancient Douglas firs and Western Red Cedars and other conifers that towered overhead. Twenty years prior, at one of the most dramatic points of the falls, a bridge had been built that let visitors safely get up close to the rampaging water. This was one of Megan's favorite spots, and she stopped there now. In times of low water the stream split here into three thready falls, but after the spring melt or heavy rains the three ribbons joined to become one waterfall, raging and spraying mist onto camera lenses and glasses and filling the air with mist. The water was high now, and the bridge somewhat slippery, so Megan clung to the railing for balance, not caring in the least as the water soaked into her clothes. For several long minutes, she stood watching the water, mesmerized as always, breathing deeply and slowly and feeling as if somehow she were a part of the breath of the earth.

The canopy of ancient trees kept out most of the sunlight, even near the path cut by the tributary, and Megan soon grew cold. She promised the waterfalls she'd return, and walked back to the more open, grassy area of the park.

While she'd been admiring the waterfalls, the crowd had grown. Certainly there weren't hundreds of people there, but there were dozens, maybe fifty or more. Megan was amazed. She'd known Romy was popular but she'd had no clue so many readers would come out to little Emerson Falls to mourn.

People were milling about without much direction, murmuring in their low tones in small groups. Many of them were carrying dog-eared copies of their favorite Rosemary Grace Garrison books. Some looked like they'd been crying; others were hugging and laughing softly as they chatted about their favorite books, characters, and scenes. Near one of the park's large open gazebos, a woman had set up a table where she was busily slipping short candles into small paper cups, to catch the wax after they were lit. Megan guessed this meant they intended to keep the vigil going at least until dark. She walked over to the woman and smiled in what she hoped was an appropriately warm but grief-filled way.

"Hi, I'm Megan," she said.

The woman stopped what she was doing and briefly shook Megan's proffered hand. "Iris," she said. "Are you a Rosette or a Romite?"

Megan tilted her head to the side. "Sorry?" she said.

"Rosette or Romite? The two main fan groups?" Iris said, as though this was something everyone should know.

"No," Megan said, shaking her head. "I live here. I'm the town librarian. What's the difference between a Rosette and a Romite?" Her wet clothes clung to her and she looked around for a sunny spot she could escape to next.

The woman picked up her task again, slipping candles into the end of the cups. "Not much, really. The Rosettes came first, and generally like Romy's earlier work better. The Romites came along later, not knowing there was already a fan club, and gave themselves a new name." She shrugged. "Sort of like Trekkers and Trekkies, I guess."

"Trekkers and Trekkies?" said Megan, thinking that there was much in this world she did not know.

"Different groups of Star Trek fans. I don't know the difference there. I'm a Rosette, but I like the Romites, too."

Uncertain what to say, Megan nodded with solemn agreement. "That's good," she said.

"I can't believe she's gone," said Iris. She paused her work. "If you live here, do you know anything about how she died? All we've heard is she drowned. Some are saying it was murder." She whispered the last word like a forbidden secret.

Megan nodded. "I don't know much myself. I think they're still working to figure it out." She took a breath: time to get sleuthing. "Do the … Rosettes and Romites, the fans, do they have theories on what happened? If it is murder, that is. They're not sure, yet." She worried that she might have said too much.

"Oh there are plenty of theories," Iris said, her voice rich with disdain. "But obviously it had to be Gus. He was so mad when she left."

Megan was surprised. From what Romy had told her, the divorce had mostly been kept out of the tabloids. How would Iris know how Gus had felt? "People think it was Gus?" she said.

"*I* think it was Gus. He lives nearby, could have gotten over here really easily. Then the next morning he'd go off to swim at eight like he does every morning, and any blood he'd had on him would have been washed off in the chlorine," Iris said.

"I don't think there was blood," Megan said, but her mind was on the last part of Iris's comment. "He swims every morning?"

"At the public pool in Concrete," Iris said, like everyone knew this and Megan was silly for asking.

"At eight?" Megan asked.

"At eight," Iris said. She glared at Megan, then coughed a smoker's cough. Megan waited patiently for the episode to subside. Finally, Iris had her breath again. "Why? You looking for a swimming partner?"

Megan shook her head vigorously. "No, no, I just …" *I just what?* An excuse didn't come to mind quickly. But already she was forming a plan in her mind to just happen to bump into the man. To see what he had to say. "Anyone else it could have been?" Megan asked, moving the conversation away from Gus.

"Well," said Iris, conspiratorially, "she's had a few stalkers over the years, of course. People who read a little too much into her books and think she's talking directly to them. She never got any restraining orders, that I heard of. As far as I know, she didn't have a stalker currently. Maybe they moved on to someone else after she ignored them too long."

"Do you know any names?" Megan asked. She was amazed at how much this group seemed to know about Romy's life. Out of the corner of her eye she saw Max had arrived, in uniform. As he'd suspected, no one was talking to him just yet. But she trusted that his dark wavy hair and his dimples and his smile would get him into a good conversation soon enough.

"Pat something," said Iris, squinting her eyes as she worked to remember a last name. "Wagner, maybe. Pat Wagner. You could look him up."

"But would he have had access to Romy's house?" Megan speculated.

"There's no security out there," Iris said. "Well, there is now. Some yellow tape, and they put a guy out there. But not until about an hour ago." She scooped the pile of candles in their cups into a box already half-full of the same, then continued making more.

Megan was taken aback. Had the fans been going out to Romy's house, then? Were they out there now, behind the yellow tape, keeping a distance but nonetheless gawking over the home that was still not quite finished? She knew Iris was correct; she remembered noticing there was no gate. There'd been no need for one, she'd thought; not out here. And obviously Romy had thought the same thing. But they'd all thought wrong.

"Okay. Well, if you hear anything that seems important, that guy over there—" she pointed to Max "—is the one to tell. Deputy Coleman," Megan said.

Iris bobbed her head. "Guy in the uniform. Got it." Her eyes lingered on Max. "He's good-looking. He's a real police? Not just a fake police?"

"A fake police?" said Megan, puzzled.

"You know, hired, for parties and such." Iris looked back at Megan and grinned salaciously, waggling her eyebrows.

"No, no," said Megan, suddenly protective of Max and her town. The influx of mourners was starting to feel like an invasion, and she wanted space to cope on her own. "Not a fake police," she said. "Anyway, nice meeting you. I'm sure Romy would have appreciated the love you all are showing." It seemed like the right thing to say. She accepted a candle Iris handed her, nodded her thanks, and headed over to Max.

As she reached him, a young woman in her twenties, with a short tight skirt and long black hair, was just walking away, a self-satisfied smile on her lips. When the woman was out of hearing range, Megan asked, "Did she give you her number?"

Max shook off the comment with a laugh. "She tried. I told her I couldn't accept phone numbers while I'm on duty."

"And she believed you?" Megan said, shaking her head at the woman's gullibility. "You're too much. Did you learn anything good?" Megan noticed Iris was watching them.

"Not yet," Max said, "but I just got here. You?"

Megan nodded in Iris's direction. "That woman over there at the table with the candles, she's sure Gus did it." Megan was about to tell Max that Gus swam every morning at eight, but then, for reasons unknown to her conscious mind, she held the information back. "Have you talked with Gus already?" she said instead.

"Yes, talked to him on Monday," Max said.

Megan was surprised he hadn't mentioned it before, but then she realized he had no obligation to tell her anything. Especially if, as he had told her, she was still a suspect herself. She felt slightly miffed that he didn't automatically know she was innocent. Wasn't that how it worked, after all? Innocent until proven guilty? And why would he suspect her at all? Sure, she'd been at the party, but then so had a lot of people. Was every one of them a suspect? Megan realized that probably they were. "Anything interesting come out of that conversation?" she asked, trying to sound as nonchalant as she could.

Max looked Megan directly in the eyes. His look was kind and reassuring, but also firm. "Nothing conclusive," he said. "He's not off the list yet, but he's not a prime suspect."

"But who else would it be?" said Megan, picking at the wax candle. "Did you find out about that Kirk Foster, the author? He seemed awfully dodgy, if you ask me." *Heebie-jeebies*, she thought.

Max drew a deep breath and nodded. "Yeah, I followed up on that. Thanks for the lead. It wasn't him. He was out of town at a writer's conference, and didn't fly into SeaTac until after the party was over, late Sunday night. He stayed at a hotel and didn't leave until morning. Hotel cameras confirm it. He's innocent."

"Oh," said Megan, disappointed. She thought momentarily that it would be nice if there had been cameras at the library that had proven her own innocence, but then decided against it. The idea of being constantly under surveillance was horrifying. Putting cameras in the public areas of the library might be something to consider, though. The library wasn't as isolated as Romy's house, but it was still far enough out that no one might hear a person scream. She shuddered at her own thought.

"You okay?" said Max, who had been watching her. "Look, I know it's upsetting that I can't tell you I've ruled you out. I just don't want to mislead you. I don't believe you're guilty. But I have to do my job."

"Oh, I know," said Megan, though really she didn't. "I understand. Don't worry about it." She looked around. "Have you seen Kevin? He was going to be here, too." She squinted into the growing crowd to try to find him.

Max scanned the crowd and found the young man first. "Over

there," he said, "by the snacks table."

Megan laughed. "Free food," she said. "I should have known. I'm going to go talk to him. I'll keep you updated."

Max put a hand on Megan's shoulder and let it linger as he held her gaze, his words unspoken.

"I know," said Megan, putting her own hand briefly on his shoulder in a mirror of his gesture, but as she walked away she realized she had no idea what his gaze had meant, or what her own words had meant in reply.

She shook off the exchange mentally and called out to Kevin as he munched on potato chips. "Hey," she said. "Fancy meeting you here."

Kevin wiped chip dust and salt from his lips and swallowed. "Hey," he said, nodding toward the table. "Free food." She remembered then how the river rafters had always been hungry because of how much physical exercise they got, and how they'd always gravitated toward free food. Zeus had been one of the worst for it. She'd always believed he had a seventh sense, an internal compass that drove him to find anything edible within a certain radius. And even if it wasn't free, Zeus usually had managed to charm people into sharing with him. He'd been the type that never had to ask for anything. People wanted him to like them, so they gave without being asked. Anything to gain favor. Acquiring free food had been the easiest thing in the world for him.

"No thanks," Megan said as Kevin held out a platter of cheese and crackers. "Have you been here long? Have you talked to anyone?"

Kevin shrugged. "I'm not sure I'm so good at this. I'm not really a talker or a listener. People don't open up to me like they do to you and Max." He topped a cracker with some havarti and shook his head. "Can you believe all these people?"

"Romy did sell millions of books," said Megan. "I guess that means more than a few people were buying." But he was right; it was surprising that so many had shown up. "Did you ever meet her? Through your girlfriend? I mean obviously you met at the party. But did you spend time with her?"

He paused. "Yeah," he said. "A couple times. She was nice. She's the person you'd need here. People would tell her anything."

Maybe that was what made Romy into a writer, Megan thought. People told her everything, and she had to do something with all the words. "What did Courtney think of her?" Megan asked. "Did she think Romy seemed depressed or anything?"

He looked up. "You mean did she drown herself? I mean, it's possible, right? Even if Max doesn't think so? Everyone's got their demons." He swept his arm wide to indicate all the people at the park. "Every one of these people, multiple demons. People think they're the only one with problems but for sure someone here has it worse than you." He ate a cracker with cheese, his thoughts far away. Watching the furrow of his brow and the way his eyes darkened, Megan thought some of his own demons might be going through his head right then.

"So what did Courtney think?" Megan repeated her question. "Did she like Romy?"

Kevin shrugged again, topping another cracker with some cheddar. "It was a job," he said. "Courtney's good at pretty much everything. Romy needed someone who could do pretty much everything, so it worked."

Megan felt him closing off to her. It was ridiculous, she thought, the way friendships, or relationships of any sort, could end. One person misreading the other, and then closing off in self-protection, which led to the other person doing the same. Neither person able to risk reaching out to see if there had been a misunderstanding. Because if there hadn't been a misunderstanding then the pain of rejection, the certainty of knowing you were no longer needed or wanted, was too much. All it would take would be for one person to reach out, but that simple act was sometimes far too much of a gamble.

She checked the time on her phone as a way to escape the conversation. "Oh gosh," she said, "I need to be getting back to the library. If you hear anything, let me know?"

"For sure," he said, and put out his hand for a fist bump. Megan steeled herself and went in for a hug instead, and was rewarded when he returned the embrace. Only briefly, but it was enough.

eight

By the time Megan got back to the library, only about an hour and a half remained before closing. The recent events had left her behind in her work, so she put her head down, dug in, and got as caught up as she could. When five o'clock came around, she was more than ready to lock the doors and head upstairs.

Much to her relief, the living quarters were quiet when she arrived. Of course if one of her guests had needed something she would have obliged, but right at the moment, she wanted nothing more than to spend some time alone.

"You still need to get to the grocery store, Megan," she said to herself as she surveyed the mostly empty refrigerator. She pulled out the leftover spaghetti to re-heat, then opened a bottle of red and poured herself a generous glass. When everything was ready she carried it out to the balcony. Noting a chill in the wind, she went back inside to get a blanket, then bundled up as she ate.

Watching the river pour by, she thought as she had many times before about how much of life took place inside one's head. Hadn't Mark Twain said something about that? She was sure he had. An observer of the scene would have seen a bucolic, peaceful sight: a young woman wrapped in a cozy plaid blanket; a hearty meal; a lovely wine. And of course, the river, always the river. If you sat and watched the river long enough, Megan thought, surely it would reach out and grab your troubles and carry them away. At least, she hoped so.

Megan's thoughts turned to Courtney. They'd met very briefly at Romy's party, but the encounter hadn't been long enough to leave Megan with much of an impression. Which is not to say she hadn't formed one already. A bit standoffish, Megan thought; Courtney carried herself with a slight air of indifference, or maybe superiority. "Or maybe she was busy thinking about party details," Megan said to the river, chastising herself for her uncharitable thoughts. Courtney had been sharp, polished; her eyes had darted around at the party, making sure all was well. "But that would have been her job," Megan told herself. Making sure all the guests who needed to be seen were seen; making sure introductions were made, making sure everything ran smoothly. "Calculating." The word slipped out of Megan's mouth. *Where did that come from?* she wondered. Maybe jealousy. Courtney seemed so put-together, while Megan often felt she was chasing her own tail to get everything done. She had no doubt Max had already talked to Courtney. Of course he had. He was good at his job, and he was fair, and he was thorough. Had Courtney been attracted to Max? "Where did *that* come from?" Megan asked the river. What business of hers was it who might be attracted to Max? "Interesting," Megan said, drinking the last of her wine.

Later, she decided there was nothing wrong with an early night, and she headed to bed shortly after nine. As was her custom now, she threw open the curtains so she could watch the sky if she woke while it was still dark. The moon would be almost full tonight, and should pass by her window as she slept.

Unusually for her, she fell asleep almost immediately, fast and hard. Dreams came quickly, the kind of dreams where she half-knew she was asleep, but still couldn't escape. In her dream, she was running in the dark through the forest path by Emerson Falls. Someone was chasing her, but the roar of the water dampened all other sounds. Faintly, she could hear someone calling for help. Was it Romy? Someone was calling for help but she couldn't tell where the sound was coming from, and the shadows of the trees tricked her into seeing ghosts that were not there. Not looking where she was going, she tripped on a tree root and fell hard on the dirt trail. Sharp rocks cut into her skin. She was bleeding and confused. Suddenly, someone was shining a flashlight in her face. The light was bright, and filled her field of vision.

Megan woke up with a gasp, her heart beating hard.

"Oh, the moon," she said with a sigh. Because the moon had risen up over the trees on the opposite bank of the river, and its light was streaming into her room, bright as a flashlight, right into her eyes. It was astonishing, the amount of light reflecting off the giant disc in the sky. Megan stared at it in wonder as her dream dissipated into the night.

Wanting to shake off the dream completely, Megan went toward the kitchen for a glass of water. Just as she passed the front door, she heard a sound down the hallway: another door closing.

She froze. Of course it would not be unheard of for one of the visitors to be entering or exiting their rooms. A glance at the clock on the wall told her it was only just past midnight. A reasonable hour for someone to be arriving home, if they'd been out. Still, all things considered, Megan felt the desire to be sure about who was in the house. Looking around, she quickly scanned the room and her mind for a weapon. "Stupid gas fireplace," she whispered, wishing for a traditional wood-burning fireplace, for which she would have had a set of iron tools, including a strong, threatening poker. A bat would be good, she thought, but she didn't play baseball. The guitar she spotted in the corner of the room—Zeus's old guitar—would make a nice sound if she crashed it over someone's head, but it wouldn't do much more.

She gave up. She grabbed her keys from the hook by the front door and slipped out without making a sound.

Even with the constant white noise of the river, everything was always so quiet out in this secluded edge of the town. Sometimes after dark, living upstairs in the library reminded Megan of the time she'd spent the night in one of the most haunted castles in England. She'd only done it to make Zeus happy; in fact, it was there that he'd proposed. She'd never admitted to him how much the idea of staying in the castle had scared her. During the day the old stone fortress was a museum, open to the public, filled with people and voices and the sounds of feet and the false digital clicks of cameras. At night, however, after everyone had gone home and the doors were locked, the atmosphere of the building had shifted. One staff person had remained, and thick red velvet ropes let the well-entrusted overnight guests know where not to roam. Megan had stepped out of the bedroom suite and into the dim interior of the castle to gaze down the capacious circular staircase, when suddenly, completely unprompted, the hairs on the back of her neck had stood on end. As if the hairs on the back of her neck knew something her eyes and brain did not. All of her cells had seemed to vibrate inside their individual microscopic boundaries, and she'd known she was not alone. She'd stepped back into the guest room where Zeus was sitting on a cushioned bench at the end of the king-sized bed, taking off his shoes. She'd gone to him and kissed him long and hard and fervently, initiating activity that ensured he would keep her mind off of ghosts for a good while. But afterwards, he'd fallen fast asleep and she'd lain awake. The thick castle walls insulated the building from all noise, leaving her in unsettling silence apart from Zeus's occasional, gentle, puffing snores. In the morning, she'd splashed cold water on her weary face, filled her gut with copious amounts of coffee to keep her awake, and said nothing.

Megan blinked hard at the memory and brought herself back to the present. She focused on the sounds of the library, but heard nothing more, whether ghostly or human.

Down the hallway, she could see a dim light leaking in through the door that should have been closed, between the apartments and the public area of the library. "Did I leave that open?" she thought, but she was sure she hadn't. She tiptoed noiselessly to the door, and willed it not to make a sound as she opened it wide enough to ease herself through.

On the other side of the door was the balcony from which the grand staircase descended into the library. Megan crept to the railing and peered down, her eyes adjusting to the low light. The river side of the main level featured many floor-to-ceiling windows to showcase the spectacular river view, and moonlight was flooding in below as it was in her own room. Megan forced her breath to be shallow and slow, so she could be as still as possible. From her elevated viewpoint she scanned the stacks and quickly noticed a light moving between the shelves, casting long eerie shadows of a person walking among them. Megan's heart leapt to her throat and she stifled a gasp. "That's the mysteries section," she thought. She looked more closely at the figure that had stopped in front of a shelf. Whoever it was, was shining the light on the books, trying to find a specific title. The light shifted, and revealed the person's identity.

"That's Sylvie," Megan said, releasing a huge sigh of relief. She walked softly down the stairs to where Sylvie was holding the book in her hands. Sylvie heard Megan approach, and looked up.

"Hi," whispered Megan. "Everything okay?"

Sylvie nodded and showed Megan the book she was holding. "*Murder by the Full Moon*. One of Romy's first. Tonight's moon made me think of it. I wanted to re-read it."

Megan then noticed Sylvie already had set the gas fireplace crackling, and had prepared the cozy reader's nook for a late night of reading. "It's a good one," Megan said. "I'll leave you to it."

"No," said Sylvie, "come talk to me for a bit. It's a little creepy down here alone." She laughed gently at herself.

Megan nodded. The enormous house took a bit of getting used to. "Of course," she said. "I'll show you a secret." She led Sylvie to the nook, where she opened up the top of an oversized ottoman in the center, to reveal a stash of fluffy throw blankets in forest greens and river blues. "I stashed these away for when I come here to read," she said, handing Sylvie a lush green throw and taking a blue one for herself. They sat in overstuffed chairs on either side of the gas fireplace and stared at it a while. Megan decided it would be best to let Sylvie lead the conversation.

"It's not real," Sylvie said, finally.

"I can't even imagine what you're going through," said Megan. "I'm so sorry."

Sylvie held up *Murder by the Full Moon*. "The sister of the murder victim in this one was based on me." She shook her head. "I was so mad at the time. The sister is not painted in the most flattering light. But probably closer to accurate than I cared to admit at the time. Romy was so astute," she said. "A keen observer. She paid attention to everything, to everyone. She wasn't really interested in sharing anything about herself. 'I already know myself,' she used to say. 'I want to understand everyone else.' No one could listen like she could. She made people feel comfortable, I guess."

"Safe," said Megan. "She made me feel safe." She saw the question in Sylvie's eyes. "When she stayed here, we talked a couple of times. You're right. I would have told her anything, probably." She reflected back on the evening she'd spent opening her soul to the author and wondered what it had been, exactly, that had made her so willing to talk. Purely and simply the fact that someone was truly interested, she decided. That had been enough. "I didn't give her the same courtesy, I'm ashamed to admit," she said.

Sylvie waved a dismissive hand in the air. "That wasn't your fault. Don't worry. That was her way. Like I said, she collected other people's stories. She didn't share hers."

Megan wished for a cup of tea or cocoa, but didn't want to ruin the mood by going to get one, even though the staff kitchen was not far away. "What was Romy's story?" she asked.

Sylvie subconsciously was running her fingers along the pages of the book, fanning their soft, well-worn edges and creating the tiniest of breezes that occasionally lifted the ends of her hair. She gazed out the tall windows at the full moon, shaping her thoughts in her mind. "Lonely," she said finally. "She was lonely." She laughed wryly. "I once told Wade that I thought Romy was lonely. He didn't believe me. He said, 'She's famous. What is she, lonely in a crowd?' I said yes. Lonely in a crowd. Surrounded by well-wishers and fans and agents and publishers, all of whom wanted something from her but none of whom really cared about her. They saw her as they needed her to be. So many of the people closest to her only wanted to be near her for what they could get from her. That feeling of being important by association." She put the book down and tucked the blanket up to her chin. "Romy didn't have a lot of friends. Too many people betrayed her early on. She stopped trusting most people after a while." The dancing light of the fire flickered in Sylvie's sad eyes, and Megan could see Sylvie had more thoughts churning, so she let the silence rest in the space between them for a while. She looked out again at the moon, bathing the river and the library in its cool glow. If she had a chance to go to the moon, would she? She'd wondered before. The problem, of course, would be the isolation. All that time alone.

"I think," Sylvie said, "I think that ultimately, everyone is lonely. Don't you?"

For a minute Megan wondered if she'd been talking out loud again, about the isolation of the moon. Then she remembered, Sylvie had been talking about Romy. "I don't know," Megan said. "I suppose maybe. Are you? Even with Wade?"

Sylvie pursed her lips and said nothing.

"My fiancé died a while back," Megan offered. "I guess there are different kinds of lonely. I have great friends, but I missed him anyway. I still do." She decided this wasn't a conversation she wanted to have right at the moment, so she turned her words back to Romy. "I've been talking to Max—Deputy Coleman. He's working so hard to figure out what happened. I'm assuming he's already talked with you?"

Sylvie nodded. "I'm not much help, unfortunately."

"Do you have any ideas at all? Who might have wanted to hurt your sister?" She looked upward, through the ceiling toward the rooms where Emlyn and Baz were staying. "What do you know about Emlyn?"

As if she'd smelled something sour, Sylvie wrinkled her nose. "She's a snob," she said, then shook her head. "But probably harmless. It's the husband who makes my hair stand on end. He never says anything but he's always there. Like a rash." She shuddered.

Megan decided that as distasteful as it might seem, she should talk with Emlyn and Baz in the morning, to see if she could get anything helpful out of them. She couldn't blame Edison for their being in the library, though; that was Lily. Lily owed her.

"What about Edison?" she said. "What was up between Romy and Edison?"

Again Sylvie was dismissive. "Oh, they were … just old friends."

"Old friends?" said Megan. "I thought they only met recently?"

Sylvie looked at Megan, as though only then realizing she hadn't been sitting there talking to herself the whole time. "No, that's right. They didn't talk about it. They met at a support group years and years ago."

The hairs on the back of Megan's neck stood up inexplicably. "They did? What kind of support group?"

"Just a general support group. Group therapy. Romy suffered from depression. Edison …" she stopped.

"Edison?" Megan said, encouraging Sylvie to go on. *What about Edison?*

Sylvie picked up the book and started flipping through the pages again. "Edison's ex-wife was abusive. Not just physically, but also emotionally. Manipulative. Cruel. Relentless. He didn't want people to know. He probably still doesn't want people to know."

This information shed a new light on things, Megan thought, but she didn't know what that light meant. Daphne Wright was capable of violence, for one thing. And Edison? What would he do to keep his past secret?

"It's just me, now," said Sylvie, opening the book. "Our parents are gone, neither of us had any kids. I'm the only one left." She switched on a lamp next to her chair and started reading.

Sensing that this was her cue to leave, Megan replaced her blanket in its secret hiding spot and headed back upstairs. She suspected sleep would not be soon in coming.

nine

As she'd expected, Megan had trouble falling asleep. Instead she lay awake puzzling over the mystery before her. "Motive and opportunity," she said to the moon as it sailed away out of view. "That's what it's about. Motive and opportunity." She went through the list of possible suspects in her head, but none seemed likely. Unlikeable, some of them, but likely to commit murder? She had a hard time believing it. Certainly she didn't want to believe anyone currently living under her roof had anything to do with it. She'd taken extra care to lock the dead bolt on her front door, but had stopped short of moving furniture in front of it—not that she hadn't been tempted.

"Emlyn and Baz," she said to the ceiling. Regardless of motive, did they have opportunity? Lily remembered them coming back to the B&B on the night of the party, and they'd been there in the morning. But Lily slept hard, and her husband, Steve, wore a CPAP machine at night, which blocked out most other sounds. Emlyn or Baz, or both of them, could have slipped out without anyone noticing a thing. "But why?" said Megan.

She checked the clock and sighed. She had plans for the morning and really wanted to get some sleep, but her mind wouldn't stop whirling. "All right, then: Daphne Wright. Or Edison," she said. Did Max know about Daphne's abusive nature? Megan hated to reveal Edison's secrets without permission, but surely that was critical information. She vowed to call the Deputy in the morning and let him know.

"None of it adds up," she said to the stars, and then she fell asleep.

* * *

The skies were dark gray and the wind was blowing the next morning as Megan set off on the mission she'd set for herself. Everyone seemed to think the prime suspect in this case was Romy's ex-husband, Gus. If Gus swam every morning at eight, well, it was a free country; what was there to keep Megan from just happening to show up at the pool and having a chat? She'd gone online and found a not-too-old picture of Gus, which she'd printed out and brought with her in the car. "I hope he looks the same now," she thought, as she pulled her car into the parking lot of the public pool in Concrete, a town near Emerson Falls.

Having no idea how long the average person might swim, she'd aimed for eight-thirty. The lot was only half full, but as she looked around she realized she had not thought this mission out particularly well. What was she going to do? Confront him? Go in and pretend she was going for a swim, in her street clothes? As she chewed on her dilemma, she sat in her car and watched the front door carefully. Two women came out, chatting and laughing with an aura of rigorous health, one with her hair wrapped in a towel and the other with her short hair still slightly damp. The door shut behind them and remained closed for a few minutes. Next, a man came out, eyes on his phone as he scrolled through calls or social media posts he'd missed. "Not Gus," Megan said, double-checking the photo she'd printed out. The man on the phone was at least twenty years younger, and his skin was too dark for it to be Gus. Another woman came out, looking at her watch and walking at a steady clip toward Megan, looking at Megan sitting in her car and making Megan's heart beat fast. Did Megan know this woman? Not intending to stare, she tried to figure out where she might have met the lady before. At the library? But the woman was staring back at her, hard, with deep concentration. She walked up to Megan's side of the car … and then continued past, to the car parked behind Megan's, got in, and drove away.

"Silly," Megan scolded herself. She then realized that while she'd been watching the woman, a man who looked a good bit like Gus had exited the pool building. She checked the photo again: bald, graying mustache, glasses, wiry body, average height. Definitely the same guy, and he was getting into his car and was about to drive away.

Megan panicked. She couldn't run over to his car now; he'd be gone before she got there. She'd just have to follow him for a bit. Most likely he'd head to a coffee shop, wouldn't he? That's what she would do after a swim, anyway. Maybe? As he pulled his car out of the parking lot she decided just to follow him and see where he went.

At first, he drove down the main roads of the town. Megan felt like a real detective, keeping her distance while holding him in sight. But shortly after, he turned up a side road with much less traffic, heading toward the hills. Megan fell back a bit, hoping not to be noticed. A few blocks later, Gus turned off onto a road that quite clearly was heading away from town.

Megan hesitated just slightly. "What would Nancy Drew do?" she said, letting Gus get a little farther away from her before turning her own car down the road. "Nancy would definitely follow him," she said. A self-satisfied smile turned up her lips as she felt quite smug. Until, that is, she realized the road was very narrow, with few places to turn around. The road curved up and up around a hill; on the right was the hill, and on the left, a steep drop-off.

She was trapped.

At which point she remembered that Nancy Drew had been kidnapped on many occasions, and suddenly Megan's plan, or lack thereof, seemed extraordinarily dense. Megan had visions of Nancy being gagged and thrown into the trunk of a car, or worse, and she wondered if her own fate might be the same. She slowed to a crawl, watching for the tiniest opportunity to turn around. But she was too late. Gus, who had apparently spotted the lone car following him down the lonely road, stopped, put his car in reverse, and backed up his vehicle until he was inches away from Megan's hood.

He got out of his car, not even bothering to shut the door, his eyes raging in anger, veins popping on his neck. He stopped at Megan's closed window, his eyes piercing through the glass at Megan's soul.

"ARE YOU THE PRESS?" he screamed. "ARE YOU THE PRESS? WHAT DO YOU WANT WITH ME? ARE YOU THE PRESS? WHY CAN'T YOU PEOPLE LEAVE ME ALONE?"

Megan had instinctively thrown her hands up in front of her face to protect herself from the man's fury. She let them down now and rolled down her window, just slightly, the car's engine still running.

"No," she said, trying to sound calm. "I'm not the press. I'm— I'm a librarian."

The words had a flabbergasting effect on Gus, who breathed hard and stared at Megan for several long seconds. "A *librarian*?" He flung his arms wide and looked around, shaking his head. "What, do I have an overdue book?"

* * *

Fifteen minutes later, Megan and Gus were seated inside a coffee shop back in Concrete. She had explained to him who she was, though she'd fudged a bit on her motive, telling him she was hoping to figure out Romy's state of mind, whether she might have wanted to hurt herself. After a bit of coaxing, Gus had agreed to talk. Much to Megan's relief, he hadn't asked her to continue along the road to his home. She was not about to get herself kidnapped and stuffed into a trunk.

Up close, Gus looked weary. Outside of the photos she'd found of him online, Megan had little way of knowing how he looked normally. But he seemed tired, like he hadn't slept for days. His shoulders slumped. He seemed capable of breathing in just enough air to keep him alive. His eyes had the look of a person who had fallen asleep crying: still somewhat puffy, but no longer red. He seemed not to have shaved all week.

It hadn't taken too much convincing to get him to come out and talk, Megan noticed. Maybe he was lonely. Maybe he needed a friend.

"I'm so sorry for your loss," she said, once the two were settled in a corner booth with their coffees and, for him, an egg sandwich.

He shook his head and shrugged unconvincingly.

Megan had rehearsed in the car what she thought she would say to Gus when she met him, but now, seeing this broken man before her, all her righteous indignation melted away. Broken was a place she knew too well.

"Today was my first day back at the pool," Gus said. Megan didn't have to ask, "first day since what?"

"That's good," said Megan. "Routine is good. Routine helps."

Gus looked up, squinting, his eyes making an accusation: *How would you know?*

"My fiancé died in a plane crash," Megan said.

The recrimination in Gus's eyes vanished. He nodded, and took another bite of his sandwich.

"Had you been in touch with Romy recently?" Megan asked. "I'm trying to sort out whether she would have hurt herself. Or who might have wanted to hurt her."

Again he shrugged, as though the effort of speaking was itself beyond him. He heaved a burdened sigh. "We didn't talk much," he said. Having wolfed down his sandwich, he now started folding a straw into a zigzag, unfolding it, and then folding it the other way, over and over and over. "But I guess I kept up on what she was doing."

Megan pondered this a minute. Did he mean he'd been stalking her? Romy had mentioned how angry he'd been with her. Megan looked around the room. Definitely she was safe here, in this public place, but one never knew who could become explosive. Zeus had always been fascinated by tales of crime on TV news magazine shows. He would go on at length about how seemingly ordinary people could just one moment be encumbered by that final straw, the last moment of sanity before they snapped into the unthinkable. Murder, he'd always said, wasn't about murder. It was about the ways people failed to cope; the ways they gave up; the ways they broke. The ways people couldn't accept the failures in their own lives, and thus tried to shift the horrible pain and the responsibility onto someone else in one irreversible, unforgivable action.

But was it unforgivable? She'd had that discussion with him many times—and it had been a discussion, not an argument, as both of them had enjoyed the philosophical discourse. In some senses, they'd agreed, it was unforgivable. In other senses, though, he had posited, in order to understand the monster outside of ourselves, we had to understand the monster within ourselves. In order to go forward with our own lives, he would say, each of us would need to let go of the bonds that anger, or the desire for revenge, could put on us.

"Any of us is capable," he would say.

"Not me," Megan would say.

"Even you," Zeus would promise, with a smile. And then he'd pull her into his lap and kiss her and tell her "I'm going to murder you with my undying affection," and make her wonder how anyone could ever kill, when there was so, so much love in the world.

A pang of missing him shot through Megan's heart.

She watched this man in front of her and thought, what does a murderer even look like? Serial killers, sure, that was one thing (Zeus would say), pathological and unmoved, but your everyday passion murderer, surely that was just an ordinary person who had snapped? She waded cautiously. "Sylvie told me Romy suffered from depression sometimes—" Megan said.

Gus jerked his head to the right. "No," he said. "She wouldn't do that."

"Then who?" Megan said.

Gus laughed. "The cops have already been out to talk to me, lady. It wasn't me. I told that cop, the one that looks like a Greek god. It wasn't me."

For a second Megan thought he meant Zeus; then she remembered: Max.

"Someone was writing big checks on her account. Have they followed up on that? Seems to me that's a place to look," Gus said.

"Someone other than Romy?" asked Megan. This was new.

He lifted his shoulders, then let them fall. "Just lots of big checks, that's all I know. That officer asked me if I had access to her bank accounts. I assumed that meant they were wondering about someone other than Romy." He rubbed his hand over his face. "She didn't care about money. Never did." He looked out the window. "Maybe she just started giving it away."

Gus's shoulders started to shake, and at first Megan thought he was laughing. Enough, she thought. A woman is dead and he's laughing? She almost got up to leave. But then she realized he wasn't laughing; he was crying. Enormous, heaving, heart-wrenching silent sobs with occasional noisy gulps of air, tears starting to stream down his face. The onslaught came on like a waterfall over a broken dam, and then subsided just as quickly. He shook his head to compose himself; pulled a mono-grammed handkerchief out of his pocket and wiped his eyes and face.

"You assume you'll have time to make amends," he said. "You just assume that one day you'll have that conversation that you've been meaning to have, that you gotta have one day, but you put it off. You make excuses, you know? You tell yourself she's not ready to hear it yet. You tell yourself she doesn't deserve your forgiveness. But that's just an excuse to put off telling her the things you wanted to tell her." He wiped his face again, then carefully folded the handkerchief and slipped it in his pocket. "She hated me. I'm probably the number one suspect because everyone knew she hated me and they thought I hated her, too. It was far easier to let everyone assume I hated her than to admit I'd been an ass. Admit I was wrong. 'One day,' I thought, 'One day I'll tell her I'm sorry and I still love her and I hope she has a good life and I hope she finds someone who can love her like I never could.' And now she'll never know." He hung his head, the sorrow bursting from deep in his soul.

A few other people in the coffee shop were watching Gus's breakdown. Of course they knew who he was, Megan thought. Everyone here would know. *The man whose famous ex-wife died,* they'd be thinking. *Probably he's pretending to be sad so they won't arrest him,* they would tell their friends. Megan glared at the gawkers until they looked away in shame. "She didn't hate you," she said quietly. She was unsure of her place in talking with him about his relationship, but his agony was too much to bear. "She talked about you with me, briefly. She said it would be easier if you were a jerk, but you weren't. That you were a good guy. She saw you."

He looked up, his eyes glistening with anguish but also hope. "She said that?" He looked out the window. The rain had returned and was coming down in sheets. He nodded almost imperceptibly. "She always did see people. That was part of what I couldn't deal with. She saw me, she saw everyone. She saw too much. It was a gift that I couldn't handle." He pulled a napkin from the dispenser and wiped his eyes. "I wasn't ready to be seen."

Megan knew this feeling, from just that short time she'd spent with Romy. "She saw me too. I wanted to be seen. It was amazing, having someone listen. And hear," she said.

Gus pulled out another napkin and wiped his nose, stuffing the used napkin in his now-empty coffee cup. He laughed wryly. "She'd listen. And then she'd turn around and put it into her books. Half the books, if you knew, you'd see me in the villain." He was quiet a moment. "I guess I deserved it."

"It's awful," Megan said. "Those conversations you never had. I know all about that. They eat at you. All the things unsaid, undone, all of it. You have to just let go, eventually."

Gus looked up. "Your fiancé," he said. Megan nodded. "Did you have unfinished business with him?"

Megan sighed to release the intense pressure that had suddenly built up in her chest. "I mean, there's always unfinished business, isn't there? The fact is," she hesitated just a moment, caught up in the camaraderie of a fellow wounded being. "The fact is, he died because of me. Not directly, but he wanted to learn to fly because he wanted to surprise me. And he wanted to surprise me because I'd told him I was worried we were getting too settled and we weren't even married yet. But it wasn't him I was worried about. It was me. Boring old librarian. He was exciting. He ran rivers and flew planes. He was extraordinary. I was scared one day he would decide I was too ordinary, and leave me. But I put it on him. And he went off to learn to fly, and he died." She peeled a napkin off the pile and wiped the tears that were starting to fall.

"How do you know he wanted to surprise you, if he died?" Gus asked.

"He'd told his parents. They told me." She felt a rush of blood, of shame, rise up her face, clear up to her hair. Zeus's parents didn't seem to blame her; still, she couldn't help but blame herself. And she had never fully faced it. "I'm sorry," she said. "I can't."

Gus reached across the table and clasped her hand. "I understand," he said.

ten

Megan had intended to stop at the grocery store on her way home; the store in Concrete had greater variety than the much smaller one in Emerson Falls. But she and Gus ended up talking quite a while longer, and by the time they parted ways she was just barely able to walk in the library doors before it opened for the day at noon. She gave a nod to her co-workers, who had been bearing the brunt of her mental and physical absence the last few days, put her coat on the back of her chair, and started work.

By the time five o'clock came around, she was starving. "Rae's it is, then," she said to her computer as she turned it off. Grabbing her coat, she raced through the rain to her car and drove over.

"Megan!" a voice called out as she walked through the door at the warm and familiar pub. A burst of joy came over Megan as she realized how much she was grateful for this local gathering spot. Several people she knew were already present, and Megan looked over their plates to see what Rae was offering up for the night. "Looks like sloppy joes?" she said to Max, who was the one who had called her name. She put her wet coat on the back of a chair at the bar, pulled out another, and sat.

"Rae's secret sauce," he said with a smile, tapping the meal on his plate with his fork. The meat spilled generously over the bun; there was no hope of eating Rae's sloppy joes like sandwiches. Megan swiped a french fry from Max's plate and dipped it in the thick gravy.

Rae came out of the kitchen carrying plates of sloppy joes for three other customers. She spotted Megan, and with their eyes and nods Rae and Megan exchanged the message that Megan would have what they were having.

"Max," Megan said, absconding with another fry. "So, I saw Gus today."

Max raised his eyebrows as high as they would go. "You did what?"

"I wasn't in any danger," Megan protested, choosing to ignore the fact that at one point she'd been worried she'd end up bound and gagged in Gus's trunk. "I didn't go to his house or anything."

The look on Max's face suggested he hadn't even thought of that possibility. "I should hope you didn't go to his house. You just happened to run into him?" He scolded her with his eyebrows. "You know I've already talked to him."

"I know, but…" Megan sighed. "Anyway, that doesn't matter. We talked a long time. We had some common ground you, know, losing someone we loved."

The disapproving look on Max's face softened and he nodded.

"So we talked," Megan continued. "Anyway, he mentioned that you told him Romy wrote out some unusually large checks in the last few months."

This time the look on Max's face, as he continued to eat his sloppy joe, was the look of someone who would neither confirm nor deny. "Go on?" he said.

"Nothing," Megan said. "It just seemed odd. He thought it was odd. I was wondering if you were looking into that."

The glittering smile, with a touch of amusement, returned to Max's lips. "I am looking into that," he said. "Oddly enough, I thought of that too." He winked. "Say, do you happen to know how long your guests are planning to stay?" he asked.

"My guests?" said Megan. It had occurred to her that morning that she hadn't been much of a hostess. Then again, she wasn't Lily. These weren't paying guests. These were people who had been foisted upon her without her having much say in the fact. "I have no idea. Saturday is the memorial for the family, I think. I'll ask Sylvie next time I see her." Even as she said it, she thought it sounded quite callous. *I know your sister just died, but can you please leave?* She decided she'd check in with her "guests" the next morning to see if they needed anything. Maybe she'd find out more then.

"Have you talked to Courtney?" Megan said, noticing her stomach was growling and hoping her own sloppy joe would come soon. "She was as close to Romy as anyone, physically, at least. You'd think she'd have some clue. Surely she has some ideas."

Max's eyes lit up with mischief. "You know," he said, "I was turned down for a K9 unit. Maybe you'd like to be my partner instead?"

Megan punched the Deputy lightly in the arm. "Come on," she said. "I'm helping. You know I am. I'm quite helpful."

"You should become an investigator," Max said. He took the last bite of his sloppy joe and wiped his lips.

Rae finally arrived with Megan's dinner and set it down in front of her. "You're becoming an investigator now?" Rae said. "Not busy enough with the library?"

"You guys laugh, but in high school when we all took those aptitude tests, mine said I should be a forensics investigator. It could have been my destiny," Megan said. She cut her sloppy joe into several pieces and took a bite. "Delicious, Rae," she said.

"A forensics investigator!" said Rae. "What made you become a librarian instead?"

"Blood and maggots," Megan said, wiping the gravy from her lips.

* * *

On her way home, Megan finally managed a stop at the small Emerson Falls grocery store. "I should get something nice for everyone," she said to the milk in the refrigerated section, and then went on a search for some baskets and treats she could pull together: cookies and teas and whatever struck her eye as nurturing and thoughtful.

As she was waiting to pay at the counter, the bells at the front door jingled and Courtney walked in. Megan saw Courtney first. She studied the young woman. Her long, extremely straight blonde hair was parted in the middle, a look that Megan thought only beautiful young women could pull of. Courtney fit the bill in that regard. Her clothes were impeccable and well made; the casual jeans were high-end, as were the black boots that peeped out from under them. Her leather jacket was perfectly tailored, and her purse had an emblem on it that Megan supposed she'd recognize if she recognized that sort of thing. Courtney quickly found a bottle of wine from the small refrigerated section and stepped up to the counter behind Megan.

"Courtney," Megan said, smiling, then she realized the young woman was giving her a blank look. "I'm Megan. The librarian." Courtney continued to stare, indifferent. "I'm Kevin's friend," Megan added, which at least got a glimmer of recognition. "I'm so sorry about Romy." The words she might say tumbled over in her mind, but none of them seemed right. Finally, she settled on: "How are you?"

"I'm fine," Courtney said, placing the bottle of red on the counter, even though Megan wasn't done paying for her order. "Looking for a new job," she said. "If you hear of anything."

"Of course," said Megan, frowning. Was Courtney really so uncaring that her main concern was her new job? "I'll keep my ears open. What sorts of things are you good at?"

Courtney gave Megan the once-over, her eyes traveling slowly from Megan's head to her toes and taking everything in: the old but comfortable clothes, the pile of frozen meals she was buying, the gift baskets and teas, the long hair Megan had pulled into a haphazard ponytail after the rain had done all the damage it could do to what had started out as a reasonably good hair day. Courtney's scrutiny seemed to Megan the closest a person could come to rolling their eyes in disdain without actually rolling their eyes. She thought Courtney was going to deem her not good enough for an answer, but then the young woman tossed her head and seemed to decide she may as well speak. "Organizing. Personal Assistant stuff. I'm good at Graphic Design stuff too, but no one around here would need that sort of work."

Megan wasn't sure what that meant, exactly, and she felt her chest puff up a bit in defense of her town. "Sure. Well, if I hear of anything I'll let you know. Are you staying with Kevin?" she asked.

Courtney pulled a twenty-dollar bill out of her wallet and slapped it on the counter. "Sometimes," she said. She caught the eye of the clerk, nodded down at the bill on the counter, and walked out the door.

"Well that was a lovely chat," Megan said. She picked up her bags and raced out again into the rain.

* * *

As Megan was unlocking her front door, she glanced down the hallway and noticed the door that led out into the library was open. She looked around, pausing to listen for any sounds of movement in the guest rooms. The library was closed, and the doors below would be locked. Megan didn't want to shut the door on any of her visitors, locking them out of their rooms. At the same time, she didn't like the idea of the door being open all night. "There's no reason to worry," she said to the corridor, but she could hear how unconvinced she sounded. After a pause, she headed down the hall, pulled the door shut and checked that it was locked. "If someone needs to get in, they can knock," she said, and she let herself into her own apartment.

After putting away her groceries, Megan looked at the piles of treats she'd gotten for Sylvie and Wade, Emlyn and Baz. The Emerson Falls grocery store was not known for its wide selection any more than it was known for its low prices. Spread out across her dining room table, the goodies seemed sparse. Megan chewed her lip, then started poking around her own house for items to supplement what she'd bought. Coming across her wine rack, she paused to consider adding bottles of wine to the assortment. "This is not a celebration," she scolded herself. "Wine is not appropriate." She pulled out her cell phone and dialed Lily. "Hey," she said when Lily answered. "Can you come over?"

Twenty minutes later, Lily was at Megan's door carrying a small bag filled with gifts she'd gathered up. As Megan let her in, she met Lily's eyes with a look of despairing gratitude. "I have no idea why I needed to get them presents, but once I looked at what I bought, it just felt woefully inadequate. I knew you would save me." She took the bag from Lily and put it on the table.

Lily smiled as she shrugged out of her jacket. "No problem at all. I keep tons of little trinkets on hand. You never know what will make someone's day." She went to the bag and started pulling out what she'd brought. "Lavender potpourri," she said, holding one packet to her nose and inhaling deeply. "So calming. I love these." She set them down. "Some lemon rosemary shortbread cookies I made this afternoon," she said, producing two small zippered bags filled with the cookies. She reached into the bag again. "Bath bombs," she said, with a frown. "I wasn't so sure. Relaxing, but not everyone takes baths." She set them down on the table. "And aromatherapy soaps," she said, pulling four small soaps from the bag. "Eucalyptus and peppermint for stress relief, and vanilla and patchouli for comfort." She sniffed one of each, closing her eyes as she drew in the scents. "Mmmm. I love those, too. That's all I brought. You said not to go overboard." Her raised eyebrows asked: is this enough?

"This is all perfect," said Megan. She handed Lily a glass of wine. "Come sit with me. Can you stay a bit?" She started toward the living room, knowing Lily would follow. She tucked herself into the corner of her couch, pulling a blanket over her legs. Lily did the same in the other side of the couch.

"I can't stay long," said Lily. "Steve is heading out of town tomorrow and I need to prep breakfast myself. But I can stay a bit. How is everyone holding up here?"

"I haven't really talked to anyone much," Megan admitted. "I mean, I don't know what to say. I'm not even sure what I'm supposed to be doing with them. They're adults. They seem to be coming and going fine. If they need me, they know I'm here." She remembered the open door. Probably something she should mention to them tomorrow, but she wasn't sure how to bring it up: *I know someone you care about has just been murdered, but can you close the door behind you?* It seemed petty, even if she knew it wasn't. They might feel safe enough to leave doors unlocked and open, but she didn't.

"I saw Courtney today," Megan continued. "At the store. She's not terribly friendly, is she?"

"Hm," said Lily. She was the kind of person who always looked for the best in others. Finding fault was not her habit. "Well," she said, "she was busy when I saw her at the party. So maybe that's it." She paused, like a thought had occurred to her, but then smiled and took a sip of wine.

"What?" said Megan, who had noticed the hesitation.

"Nothing," said Lily. "Just remembered something I'd forgotten. Nothing important."

Megan shrugged it off. "I saw Gus today, too," she said. "Romy's ex-husband."

"Oh?" said Lily, her interest piqued. "Was he in town?"

"Uh, well," said Megan, "some judgmental people might say I stalked him. Which would not be true. I happened to be outside the pool in Concrete when he got done with his morning swimming. Whatever. Why I was there is not important."

Lily gently shook her head as her eyes laughed.

"Anyway," said Megan, "something he said. I didn't think much of it at the time, but it just occurred to me that I keep hearing this. He talked about how Romy was such a good listener—and then she'd take what she'd heard and write it into her books. Sylvie said Romy based a character in one of her early books on Sylvie. Or maybe it was more than one. I can't remember. But my point," she said, waving her glass of wine in the air to punctuate the fact that she did, in fact, have a point, "my point is, what if that was Romy's common practice? And what if one of the people whose stories she listened to, didn't very much appreciate having their story fictionalized?"

"Interesting," said Lily. "Very interesting. But how would we even know? There's no way to know who all Romy talked to in her life, and we'd have to know that in order to match books up with their origin stories."

"Maybe …" said Megan.

"Yes?" said Lily. "You have an idea?"

"Well, it's just … I mean, don't be going around telling people," Megan said, but the words were just precautionary. Lily was the most discreet person she knew. "Apparently Romy and Edison met a long time ago. At a support group."

Lily raised her eyebrows. "Oh?"

"Romy was dealing with depression. And Edison was dealing with the fact that his wife was abusive."

This news was clearly a surprise to Lily. "Nooooo. Daphne?" she said. "The ex-wife?"

"Yes," said Megan. "Did you ever meet her?"

Lily squinted, looking back in her memory. "Maybe. Just in passing. I feel like I might have but I couldn't be certain."

"Well," said Megan, "regardless, it sounds like Edison didn't want people knowing about all that. Which is why he made up the story that he met Romy at some author event. I'm just thinking, what if he found out she wrote about him, and he thought the story seemed too thinly veiled, and he was embarrassed? Or if Daphne was violent, and she thought people would be able to tell that the story was about her. Would that be a trigger?"

Lily looked around. "Where's your laptop?" she said, putting her wine glass down. "I can't remember all of Romy's books, but I've read most of them."

Megan ran into her bedroom to get her laptop, turning it on as she came back into the room. "I've read many of them, but not all." She pulled up a list of all the books Romy ever wrote, and the two started going down the list from the beginning, recalling the basic plots as best they could. After about thirty titles, they were starting to feel the futility of the effort. Then they got to *Death of a Social Butterfly.*

"Wait," said Lily. She read the description. "'When a rich socialite turns up dead in her own pool, everyone believes it's suicide. But the story takes an unexpected turn when her dark past is brought to light.' I remember this one. The husband did it, because the wife beat him and he'd finally had enough." She looked at Megan, her mouth open. "Do you think...?"

A chill ran up Megan's spine. She checked the time: ten-thirty. Too late to call Max with nothing more than a suspicion, based on a coincidence in a book Romy wrote years ago. She remembered then that she was living in Edison's old home; she remembered how she used to think about the ghosts that seemed to live there, even though the house wasn't old enough for ghosts. Could they have been ghosts of a different kind? Ghosts of the memories of the fights and violence? Megan looked at the walls, as though they held secrets. Maybe they did, she thought. Maybe they did.

Then she remembered Edison's words to her: *If those walls ever start to talk, you'll understand.*

Was that what he'd meant? Was he talking about the abuse he'd suffered here, in this house, at Daphne's hands?

She shuddered.

"Daphne's alive, right?" said Lily. "Daphne's not actually, secretly, Romy? Do we know for sure that Daphne and Romy are two different people? I mean, in the book it's the wife of the abused guy who ends up dead. Maybe ...?"

"Of course they're two different people," Megan said, but her tone held no certainty. Where was Daphne, after all? "No, Romy was married to Gus for ... well, decades. She couldn't also be Daphne."

Lily lifted her shoulders. "You hear those stories about people who live two lives. Carrying on living in two towns, two families, two homes, and they get away with it for years. You never know," she said.

"There is no way Romy lived two different lives and also wrote two or more books a year. Just impossible," Megan said. But was it?

Lily closed the lid on Megan's laptop. "Well, regardless, I need to get going. Breakfast comes early at the inn," she said. She stood and wrapped up again in her coat.

"Text me when you get home," Megan said, as she walked Lily to the door.

"I will do so," said Lily. "Now don't worry about it. Lock the doors and get some sleep."

"So very comforting," said Megan. She gave Lily a hug and sent her on her way.

Coming back into her house, she remembered the gift baskets. She quickly piled all the gifts she'd bought into the baskets, along with the much more appealing additions Lily had brought, then took them out into the hall to place outside the doors of her guests. As she returned to her own apartment, she noticed the door to downstairs was open again, and a soft light filtered through. Megan tiptoed to the grand staircase and peered down into the space below. There, she saw Sylvie sitting by the fireplace. She held a book in her hand, but her eyes were lost in the fire, lost inside a memory she could never live again.

eleven

Megan slept poorly, her night filled with bizarre dreams. She dreamed that she was herself and Romy and Daphne all at once, but nobody could see her anywhere she went. She had two husbands, one of whom was Gus. In her dream she called the other one Edison, but when she woke, she realized the face on the man had been that of Zeus. And in her dream, she had beaten him. She hadn't been able to feel the blows as her hands landed on his body, but his blood pooled in bruises under his skin as he looked on with pleading, begging eyes. Finally, in an act of self-preservation, Edison/Zeus pushed back, and she fell, face-first, into a pool. She didn't struggle. She breathed the water into her lungs, welcoming the end, letting the cool liquid fill her until there was no air left in her, only water and blood. Slowly, she sank to the bottom of the pool, looking up through the wavy depths to see Edison/Zeus looking down at her, yelling out at her something that she couldn't hear. From the bottom of the pool she calmly watched his mouth in its screaming frenzy. Then the blood from his bruises spilled over into the water, darkening it, blotting out all light until she could no longer see.

She woke up in a pool of sweat.

The moon was waning but again its light was shining in her window whispering secrets she couldn't understand. Wisps of low clouds floated past the moon and wove themselves through the shadows of the treetops. The river sighed and hummed on its never-ending journey from the mountains to the Puget Sound. A hush lay over the world.

Megan lay awake in the dark for a while as her mind tried to sort dream from reality. "None of this is happening," she said to the moon. If only that were true, she thought.

Soon, she fell back asleep. She did not dream again.

* * *

When she next woke, the day was already dawning to bright sunshine. Groggily, Megan tried to recall what day it was. "Friday," she finally said to the room. The memorial would be tomorrow. Then, she hoped, she would have her home to herself again.

Still in bed, she stretched and snuggled into the blankets. April nights were cold enough that she hadn't switched from her flannel sheets yet. These sheets, soft and warm in her favorite buttercup yellow that felt bright even in the depths of winter, had been a gift to her from Zeus three years before. They were starting to get threadbare in places, but Megan couldn't part with them. Logically, of course, she knew that there was nothing in the sheets of Zeus that wasn't in her heart and mind. But still she clung to them as if that meant she didn't quite have to say goodbye. "Maybe next winter," she said out loud to the sheets, and she sighed.

"Okay!" she said with determination. "Time to get up." She flung off the sheets and sat on the edge of the bed. "What is our game plan today?" She looked around the room and thought how Zeus would have laughed at its extravagance. He had been a simple man with simple needs. A tent, a thermos, a campfire. Maybe a thin pad under his sleeping bag, if he was feeling fancy. Anything more than that was more than any person needed, he'd say. But in secret, Megan knew, in secret he'd loved a good lush bed as much as she did. The flannel sheets had not been just for her. She would wake up and see him next to her, surrounded by the soft yellow, and in the candor of sleep his face would be wearing a smile of peace.

"I wish you were here now," she said, looking at the pillow on the other side of the bed. She wanted to talk to Zeus about Romy, about the house full of strangers, about Gus, about how relationships fell together and how they fell apart. She wanted to hear his thoughts on Edison and Daphne and how their life turned stereotypes on their heads. She wanted to trade insights on how that might have made Edison feel, how shame could maybe lead a person to crime.

She just wanted to talk to him again, about anything.

Megan's balcony beckoned to her, so she quickly prepped a breakfast of oatmeal with a topping of berries and some chia seeds. Oatmeal in one hand and a hot mug of coffee in the other, she headed outside. Her Adirondack chair was coated with a thin morning dew, so she headed back inside for a towel. After wiping down the chair, she sat and planned out her day.

"The guests," she said, watching the steam rise from her coffee. She should stop by and check on them, see if they needed towels or laundry or anything. It occurred to her that if she was going to have guests on a regular basis, it might not be a bad idea to see if the library board, or Edison, would consider installing a washer and dryer upstairs that guests could use. Item number one on her list for the day: check on the guests.

"And then?" she asked the river. It was still running high from the spring rains. This would have been one of Zeus's favorite times of the year. It had seemed to Megan that higher water should mean a calmer river, but Zeus had told her the truth was just the opposite. Most river rafting companies wouldn't run rafting trips when the water was this high. On a day like today, Zeus would have been out early to get the best routes all to himself.

Megan shook her head to bring herself back to the present. "And then," she said, "Edison." With her new idea of installing the washer and dryer, she'd have a reason to talk to him. How to bring the conversation around to the book Romy wrote, though, the one that seemed to have been based on his life? Well, she'd worry about that later. For now, she'd worry about housekeeping. Literally.

Half an hour later, Megan was showered, dressed, and in the hallway outside her door. A quick glance told her that Sylvie and Wade had found their gift basket, but Emlyn and Baz must have not yet stepped outside. Megan suspected Sylvie would have picked hers up on her way back in from her night down-stairs in the reading nook. She decided to head to their room first.

Almost a minute passed after Megan knocked before Wade answered the door. He was dressed impeccably, crisp white shirt and khaki pants, no tie, polished shoes, looking ready for a day at work. "Yes?" he said. There was no unkindness to his tone, but neither was he welcoming.

"I, uh, I was just wondering if you needed anything," Megan said.

Wade took in her question as though it was being run through a translator before entering his ears; like he was waiting, pa-tiently, for her words to make sense. "Do we need anything?" he said, finally. Calm, passive, indifferent.

"Like, new sheets or towels or anything." Megan suddenly felt awkward, but Wade's face changed to understanding and he nodded.

"Oh, yes. If you could leave us some new towels and sheets, I think Sylvie would like that," he said. "Just leave them outside the door." He paused. "You were the one who left the basket," he said, as though he'd just realized where the assortment might have come from.

"Yes," said Megan. "I ... well, I'm not sure what to do in ... this situation. I wanted to let you know I was thinking of you."

Wade nodded again. His silence drew out long. Megan wondered if he always spoke like this, taking his time with the words on their way in and their way out. How could Sylvie stand it? Megan wasn't sure she'd be able to. She'd want to jump in and give him the words she expected, or maybe needed. Sylvie must have the patience of a saint. "It is not a usual situation," Wade said. Again he nodded, and it seemed to Megan he was agreeing with thoughts before releasing his words into the world. "We appreciate the gesture."

"Of course," said Megan. "You're welcome."

Wade didn't answer, but stood looking at her. He'd seemed warmer at dinner the other night, but now he was closed off. Megan imagined the strain must be getting to him, as it was to her. She looked at him more closely and noticed a weariness in both his face and in the slight slump of his shoulders.

"So, just leave the dirty towels and sheets outside the door, and I'll, uh, come get them," Megan said, "after I leave you new ones of course." With every passing day she felt more like she was earning her keep in this spectacular home. It did not, it seemed, come without a price. "If you need anything else," she said, and she leaned her head toward her own apartment, indicating: you know where to find me.

Wade nodded. Megan blinked and imagined him as a bobble-head doll. Just in time, she stopped herself from telling him to have a great day. A great day was probably not what one had just a few days after one's sister-in-law was murdered. She nodded in return, and walked away as he closed the door.

At Emlyn and Baz's door, Megan first stooped to pick up the basket that was still waiting outside. She knocked. Emlyn took even longer to get to the door. She, in contrast, was still in her pajamas and bathrobe, her face shiny with a night moisturizer she hadn't yet washed away.

Emlyn said nothing, but looked at the gift basket in Megan's hands, her critical eyes scrutinizing it and Megan much in the way Courtney's had.

"Good morning, Emlyn," said Megan, brightening her voice to make up for Emlyn's lack of enthusiasm. "I thought I'd come by and see if there's anything you need? Towels or sheets or anything?"

"Oh yes," said Emlyn, opening the door wider, indicating Megan could come in. "Now's fine."

Megan realized Emlyn thought Megan was offering maid services; that she'd strip the bed and gather up the towels herself. *That is not going to happen*, she thought, setting her mind even though much of her thought it would be easier just to give in. "Oh, I didn't bring them with me," Megan said, her tone a little less bright and her kindness a little more forced. "I'll bring them by and leave them outside the door for you. You can leave the used linens out here and I'll pick them up." She looked around the room. Dirty clothes and discarded shoes lay on the floor where they'd fallen. A crumpled towel had been abandoned across the back of a wooden chair, making Megan shudder internally as she hoped it wasn't wet and leaving a mark. Papers were strewn across the small desk, including a very thick stack held together by a giant, bright red binder clip. A laptop sat on the unmade bed, a browser page open to what seemed to be some sort of celebrity gossip page. "Has Baz gone out already this morning?" Megan asked. The bathroom door was open, and no one else was in the room.

"He left Wednesday," said Emlyn coolly. "He had to work." Now that she realized Megan wasn't going to clean up, she started to close the door.

Megan felt herself blushing. Could she have noticed Baz was gone? Should she have noticed? It wasn't as if anyone was required to check in with her. Another point to bring up with Edison when she talked with him: this guesthouse was going to need some rules and guidelines. "Oh, I see," she said. She placed the gift basket on the small table just inside the door. "Just some things I thought you might like," she said. "I'm sorry I haven't checked in before." She wanted desperately to ask Emlyn if she'd be leaving soon, too, but she couldn't think of a way to phrase it that wouldn't offend. "You're staying for the memorial tomorrow?" she asked.

"Through tomorrow, then flying back east on Sunday," said Emlyn. "I've got Romy's last book and the publisher wants it out as soon as possible."

Megan felt a surge of relief. Now if she could just get Sylvie and Wade to leave, too .... She felt awful the moment the thought crossed her mind, but still, she would be glad for them all to be gone.

"I hope you have a safe flight," Megan said. "I'll be here if you need anything. I'll drop off the towels and sheets later."

"That's fine. Have a nice day," Emlyn said, and closed the door. The way she said it made Megan feel she was not entirely concerned with whether Megan actually had a nice day.

"You too," Megan said to the door. She headed down the hall to a closet that held extra linens, toilet paper, and the like, for the guest rooms, pulled out the clean sheets and towels, and left them outside the guest room doors without knocking again. "They'll find them," she said under her breath, feeling slightly guilty but also slightly defiant. She was a librarian, not a house-keeper.

And to that end, she decided to give Edison a call. Back in her own kitchen, she rang him up, and he answered immediately.

"Megan!" he said, his enthusiasm almost startling her in its contrast to Wade and Emlyn. "What can I do for you?"

"Hey, Edison," said Megan, feeling herself smile at his warmth. How could a person not like Edison? Her mind wandered briefly to his ex-wife, Daphne. How could she have wanted to hurt this kind man? But the book, she thought. *Death of a Social Butterfly*. Stay focused. "Say, are you around this morning? I have some library thoughts and if you have time …."

"Sure!" said Edison quickly. "I'm just back from my run. Into the shower and then I can come over. Will that work? Conference room over there? Maybe downstairs? I like the view. I miss that view, to be honest. The house was too much but the view was great." He spoke quickly, like his words could chase something away.

Megan felt like her heart was beating faster just to keep up with him. "That's perfect," she said. "I'm ready whenever you are. Just buzz and I'll come on down."

"See you in about thirty," Edison said, and the line went dead.

Megan looked at the phone in her hand. Should she be offended by the fact he hadn't even said goodbye? Megan decided to chalk it off to his high energy, and let it go. She looked at the time—just after nine—and went off to make a sweep of the library before heading to the basement level to meet with Edison.

The morning was quiet. She loved this time in the library, when she could be alone and imagine that the public library was all hers. She breathed in deeply as she descended the grand staircase. Even though the library had only been open a short time, already the musky smell of old and new books gently permeated the air. From halfway down the stairs she could see over the tops of all bookshelves—or the "stacks," as they called them in the library business. She recalled the conversation she'd had with Romy about how every book held a part of someone's mind; how a library was like a room full of brains. When she was younger, Megan had thought that if she could have a superpower she'd want to be able to talk to the characters in books. Have conversations with them and be their friends. Make them come to life. She knew some of the characters in her favorite books so well that they felt like long-lost companions. The fact that she couldn't actually ever talk with them in real life had frustrated her to no end back then. And still now, even, sometimes. Megan once joked to Zeus that she didn't fully trust anyone who hadn't at some point secretly wished for their own letter from Hogwarts. "You're a wizard, Megan," Hagrid would say, and she'd be swept off to a place where magic was real and everything was possible. Who wouldn't want that? Or who wouldn't want to visit Middle Earth (perhaps minus Sauron or Smaug the Impenetrable) and have second breakfasts with the hobbits? Who wouldn't want to walk through the back of a wardrobe and find a whole other world?

Megan smiled to herself as she walked through the stacks, lining up the spines of the books and pulling anything that was out of place. Every section—whether non-fiction, biography, children's, general fiction, all of it—every section had its own aura, she thought. Biography made her think about courage and the strengths and frailties and common struggles of humanity. Non-fiction made her think about the passing of time and all the things she wanted to do in life. The children's section brought on nostalgia for an innocent age she could never regain. Adult fiction reminded her of authors' delightful, irrepressible imaginations. If asked, Megan could wax rhapsodic about the invention of language and about communication and how, above all else, humans need stories as much as humans need air.

She sighed with deep contentment. In so many ways, this library was home.

A vibration on her phone told her Edison was at the downstairs door, and she raced down the back stairs to meet him, stopping quickly in the mystery section to pick up a copy of *Death of a Social Butterfly*. The lower level was largely the domain of Owen Scott, a young man who had grown up in the area, gone off to the University of Washington to get a degree in Philosophy, and then found himself back by the Skagit River, looking for a job. Megan had been the one to interview him, and had been charmed by him instantly. He was the kind of person who was hard to get to know, in part because he was shy and quiet about himself, but also in part because he was so attuned to the person he was talking to. He shifted all the focus off of himself in such a way that people never realized until much later that they'd only talked about themselves. And the next time he saw them, he'd remember everything: ask how that meeting had gone or how they'd liked their trip to Canada or how their mother was doing since the surgery. He was quiet and he was kind and he did his work with great care, and while the rental services were not yet booming, he nonetheless labored tirelessly over the library's social media website, making sure everyone knew about new books that came in, reminding them of the rooms available to use, or sharing photos of the river taken from his office window.

Owen was not scheduled to be at work for a couple more hours, though. The lights were off downstairs, but the rooms had been built with as many floor-to-ceiling windows as the structure would allow, and the daylight was already pouring in.

Megan could see Edison at the door, and waved through the window at him.

"Hello," she said, opening the door wide.

"Megan!" said Edison, holding out his arms for a hug but waiting to see if she was up for it. Megan decided she was, and moved in. During the brief embrace, she thought about how much she missed that, being surrounded by strong arms and a warm torso. But before she got too lost in memories, she pulled away.

"Good to see you, Edison," she said. "I thought maybe the small conference room out front? I don't mean for this to be so formal. It just seems like a nice chance to use these rooms, since the view is so great." She led the way to a room that faced the river, let him choose his seat first, and sat down. As she did, she saw his eyes settle briefly on the book in her hand. His face remained unchanged for a few long seconds, and then he looked away at the view outside. Megan tucked the book under the table onto the seat of the chair beside her.

"Lawn's looking good," Edison said. "Lots of tulips. People like that, bright and cheery flowers. Daphne even liked them. Gardeners coming in regularly like they're supposed to?"

"Yep," said Megan. "They're the best. Leo, the head gardener, has some plans for the area. There's so much space both inside and out, and we haven't yet figured out what to do with it all."

Edison's eyes glazed over just slightly as he stared out at the river. "I'd been talking with Romy about the theater idea, building a little theater out of that enormous garage. She was really into it. Thought it could be fun to have a theater named after herself. 'The Romy,' that was her suggestion. 'Come see a show at The Romy.' She had a good laugh over that one. Thought it was hilarious for some reason." He didn't laugh.

The thought passed Megan's mind that it might be a nice

thing for Sylvie to do with some of the money she would get from Romy's estate, but she decided it would be tactless to say so. "Maybe the town can do some fundraising to make that happen," she said instead.

Edison looked at her with unexpected candor. "So what's up, Megan?" he said. He seemed to be concentrating on not looking at the chair next to Megan.

"Well," Megan started, "just some thoughts on the guest rooms, first. With all these people staying here, I've noticed some things we hadn't thought about before. Like laundry. I'm happy to step in to an extent," she said, while thinking that maybe she wasn't all *that* happy about it, really. "But if people stay longer, you know, they may need to wash some things. I'm wondering if we could think about installing a washer and dryer for guests to use."

Edison had set his phone on the table, and now he picked it up: something to do with his hands. He twirled it absentmindedly and tapped it against the finely burnished wood of the table top. "We didn't expect this, did we? I suppose I thought having the guest suites up there was just a way to use up some space. Didn't think we'd turn you into a hotelier. That's not been entirely fair to you, has it?" He furrowed his brows, thinking. "We certainly can think about that. Were you thinking something near the linen closet? That's pretty big, isn't it?"

"I think that would work, yes. I appreciate that you see it's … well, unexpected is the best word for it, I guess. Maybe it's not. Horrifying is the best word. But unexpected, too."

"How's everyone doing?" Edison asked, now running his thumb around the edge of his phone.

"Well, Baz has left, I just found out," Megan said. "Wednesday. I don't know if he asked Max, or told Max. I feel bad that I didn't notice. I think Sylvie's having a rough time. She goes down to the reading area at night a lot, in the library."

"The reading area?" said Edison. "Why there?"

"It's a nice, quiet spot," said Megan. "I like to go there, too, when the library is closed. It feels … I don't know. It feels safe somehow."

Edison's eyes clouded over. "I liked to sit by those windows, too," he said. "When this was my house." He brought himself back to the present quickly. "So I'll talk with the board about laundry and what else we might need to make it easier on you when you have to be an innkeeper. I'm not here today just to talk about laundry, though," he said. It was neither an accusation nor a question; just a statement letting Megan know he knew the truth. "What's up?" His glance fell in the direction of the chair on which Megan had put Romy's book.

Megan took a deep breath. Confrontation was not her strong point, and what's more, she wasn't even sure what she wanted to ask.

Edison watched her stumble for words for a few moments, then took the plunge for both of them. "That's an interesting book you've brought with you," he said, nodding his head toward the chair.

A warmth spread up Megan's chest and neck, and the air felt close and thick. "Well, now that you mention it…"

Edison burst out with a great guffaw. "Now that *I* mention it!" he laughed. "You just happened to have that book in your hand when you came to a meeting with me that you asked for, but *I'm* the one mentioning the book?" He swirled his phone between his fingers and tapped it again on the table top. "Who told you?"

Megan cleared her throat. "Who told me what?" she asked. She genuinely wasn't sure which facts he was asking about, and didn't want to play too many unplayed cards.

"About Daphne," Edison said, leveling his eyes at Megan. "About how I met Romy." He held her gaze for an uncomfortable amount of time, but Megan didn't look away. Finally, Edison broke eye contact. As if he'd been still for too long, he stood and started pacing the room. His sudden agitation worried Megan. Had this been a bad idea? What had she been thinking, inviting a murder suspect here without someone else present? Quickly she scanned the room. The doors were unlocked. She could run if she needed to. And if he decided to block a door, well, how hard could it be to break through a windowpane? *Probably harder than you think*, she thought.

Edison was still waiting for an answer: unusual patience from this usually irrepressible man. He stopped behind a chair and leaned over slightly to hold onto on to its back, patient, like a cat waiting for its mouse.

"Well, I guess it was Sylvie," said Megan. "The other night, downstairs. Upstairs, I mean. Upstairs from here. The reading area. We were just talking about ..."

"About who killed Romy?" said Edison. He squinted his eyes. "You think I killed Romy?"

"I don't ... I don't have any idea who killed Romy."

"You think I have a motive, though. A reason to kill."

Megan paused and took a breath. "I'm just trying to figure it all out," she said.

"I heard you talked to Gus the other day, too. You're just going around playing detective?" he said.

Don't get caught up in his emotions, Megan told herself. *Stay focused*. She looked out the window, letting the flow of the river smooth the edges of her mind. "You talked to Gus, too?" she said.

"Maybe you're not the only one trying to get to the bottom of all this," he replied.

She looked at him, carefully, trying to see cues. She'd read a few books on how to tell whether people were lying. Not breaking eye contact, inability to keep their stories straight, hiding their mouths while they're talking, fumbling over their words. What else?

She studied his posture. The arch of his eyebrows. The lift of his shoulders. The tightness of his jaw. The way his green-blue eyes bore into hers. But not in an attempt to deceive her, she thought; he wanted desperately to be believed.

A wave of relief passed over her as she realized: she believed him.

"Oh, Edison," she said with a long sigh. "What happened to Romy?"

The tension drained from his face and body, leaving behind only grief and exhaustion. "I don't know," he said.

The book next to her pulled her attention. She picked it up and put it on the table. "Well, then, let's figure it out," she said. "Tell me about Daphne."

Edison shook his head. "Romy, Romy, Romy," he said, reaching for the book. "Loved that woman, but she did have a way of mining her friendships for literary fodder. Have you read this?" He flipped through the worn pages, stopping about a third of the way through and then paging through more slowly until he reached the point in the story he'd been looking for. For a minute, the room was silent as he re-read.

"I read it a long time ago," Megan said finally. "Obviously I didn't know it was about you at the time. I don't think I even knew you at the time." She watched as he continued to read. After a few more minutes, he closed the book and pushed it back across the table.

"It's not *about* me," he said. "Romy explained to me, over and over, that it was *inspired* by me. She said I could be *inspirational* to other men who were in my situation." He shook his head. "That was a load of bull. If anyone had known what was going on between Daphne and me, and if they'd known I knew Romy from our group, they would have guessed. But it wouldn't have upset me nearly as much as it would have upset Daphne. Being seen as the perfect beauty, the perfect socialite, was everything to her." He gazed around the room. "This used to be my work-out room," he said, then he paused. "Mostly she was verbally abusive. Manipulative. Threatening me and my career if I didn't give her what she wanted. Trying to keep me isolated from my friends and family. Lying about me to make me look bad. But she did like to hit me and to throw things at me." His eyes went to the corner of the room. "I kept the free weights there. She liked the three-pound dumbbells. She had pretty good aim, actually."

The words "why didn't you leave her sooner?" wanted to fly out of Megan's mouth, but she stopped them in time. Domestic violence, she knew, was complicated. And besides, that's not what they were here for this morning.

"How did Daphne feel about Romy?" she asked. "Did she know about this book?"

Again he shook his head. "As far as I know, she never found out about the book. If it wasn't a glossy magazine with pictures of celebrities and rich people in it, she wouldn't read it. She wouldn't have known. But as far as Romy, she didn't like her. Daphne was furious when I divorced her." A tiny smile curled the corner of his lips. "Especially since she got almost nothing." He looked Megan in the eyes. "Always get a good lawyer," he said.

"I'm so sorry you went through all of that," Megan said. "I don't really know what to say."

"That's just it," he said. "No one really knows what to say, if they even believe you." He shrugged. "Was Daphne capable of killing Romy? Absolutely. Did she have motive? In her mind, I'm sure she has a motive to kill just about everyone. Did she do it? That I don't know."

"You said she lives around here?" Megan said.

"Yeah, so far I haven't managed to shake her. Lives a few towns over. I try to pretend she doesn't exist."

"Was she the jealous type?"

"Was she the jealous type?" Edison repeated, laughing. "Was she! Every hair on her head was jealous. Everything anyone else had, she wanted. If she wanted something, she expected it to be given to her. She was the epitome of entitled and the epitome of jealous."

Megan pursed her lips. "If you don't mind my asking…"

Edison anticipated the question. "What did I ever see in her?" he chuckled. "We were young. I thought I knew what I wanted. I thought I knew her. I thought she loved me." He paused and looked at his left hand, where the ring once sat. "I was wrong." He leaned back and folded his arms. Megan took this as a sign not to press any further.

"Okay. Well, what about the night of the party. Did you notice anyone? Was anyone acting strange? Doing anything … I don't know … suspicious?"

At this, Edison laughed. "Well, there was that one guy carrying around a bloody axe, do you mean him?"

Megan gasped, then caught herself. "You almost got me. Okay. So there wasn't anyone doing anything overtly suspicious. But think back. Who did you see with Romy? Was anyone mad at her? Anyone glaring at her from the other side of the yard?"

"Not really," he said. "Courtney stuck by her side most of the night, and Emlyn did, too. Baz sort of wandered around aimlessly. Sylvie and Wade hung out in the house, mostly. Just a lot of well-wishers, people networking, and then the more they drank, flirting."

"What do you know about Courtney?" Megan asked. "She doesn't strike me as the warmest person."

"No," he said, leaning forward again, "but she's efficient. She took care of everything for Romy. I think Romy trusted her. She was never a micromanager, Romy. She was more than happy to have other people taking care of details for her, and Courtney was good at what she did."

"What all did she do?"

"Oh, everything and anything, I suppose. From buying groceries to managing the household to some accounting and paperwork to taking the car in when it needed repairs. Pretty much everything."

"How did Romy find her, do you know?" Megan asked.

"Ad in the paper?" Edison said. "Honestly, I have no idea. I don't know much about her. She just did her thing pretty quietly."

"Hmmm," said Megan.

"Hmmm?" said Edison.

"Just wondering about her. She had close access to Romy. But she didn't live at the house, right?" Megan asked. "Was she still at the party when you left?"

"I think so," Edison said. "I was one of the last ones out the door. She was still there cleaning up."

"Hmmm," said Megan.

"Hmmm," said Edison. "Hmmm indeed."

twelve

The library was buzzing more than usual for a Friday afternoon, and Megan kept busy in the roles of both reference librarian and Library Director. She didn't mind. Answering questions and handling the drudgery of paperwork gave her something to keep her mind off of Romy.

Besides which, Megan loved being in the library and, more specifically, at her desk. She'd been involved in selecting the furniture for the new library, and she loved this desk—the one indulgence she'd requested. It was made of cedar, delighting the eye with its light and dark variations, and it surrounded her in a large, cozy circle. It felt like her own private cave, or like living inside a giant hollow tree trunk. With the exception of a few cutouts where people could approach and ask questions, the curved sides were high. Even though she was somewhat at the center of the library, she still felt protected and safe.

And the rest of the main library space was cozy, as well. Commercial-grade outdoor string lights had been hung throughout the public area, giving the room a warm, welcoming glow that added to the relaxed, intimate feel. When people first saw the space, they often commented that they might never want to leave. Being at her desk always made Megan feel peaceful and at home, like she was somehow ensconced within a forest glen of books. It was her own personal paradise.

At some point in the early afternoon, while she was researching a question about the migration patterns of raccoons, Megan saw Wade come down the grand staircase. He headed into the staff kitchen carrying several dirty mugs, and returned a few minutes later with the handles of six clean mugs looped through his fingers. He nodded quietly at Megan as he passed, and she felt herself blush. Should she have taken care of their dishes, too? She sighed and decided she'd worry about it later. Another thing to bring up with Edison.

She was relieved to believe Edison hadn't been involved with Romy's death. Megan liked Edison. She didn't want to think she'd been wrong about him all along. He was nice. He was maybe more than nice.

As she was sorting through employees' time sheets for the month, Owen, who ran the conference services downstairs, came up to her desk. He was tall and lanky, and undoubtedly must have been gangly as a teen, a decade or so ago. His light brown hair was almost unmanageably thick, and normally he kept it cut short. Today, though, he was long overdue for a haircut, and Megan's first thought was that he could be a younger brother to the Heat Miser from that Christmas special whose name she could never remember. The Heat Miser was short and squat, she thought, but the other one, the Snow Miser, his hair wasn't right. The height of the Snow Miser, but the hair of the Heat Miser. Maybe Owen could be just a ... Luke Warm Miser. Something in between.

"Hey," Owen said, leaning over the desk to see what Megan was working on. "I got mine in, right?" He saw Megan contemplating his hair and self-consciously reached to pat it down.

Megan suppressed a laugh. Owen would not want a nickname of Luke Warm Miser. "Yours is in. Thank you. Everything good downstairs? People starting to make reservations?" she asked.

"Yeah, Betty and Carol Louis-Lewis want to reserve the space for a party for their grandson. They were asking about using the yard, too. The grandson has a summer birthday and they thought it would be nice to have the party both inside and outside," he said.

"Hmmm," said Megan. "I don't know why not, but I suppose I'll have to run that one by the board." She made a note on a pad of paper. "I'll let you know. Any others?"

"Helen and Dave Hofstetter, also wondering about outside space. Their twenty-fifth anniversary is coming up. Dave was going to try to surprise Helen with a party but he needed her help to plan it," he laughed. "So it's not a surprise anymore. Anyway, they wondered if they could bring tables to set up outside. This is for August."

Megan made another note. "Okay, I'll email the board and let them know we want to talk about that. I have a few other things I need to bring up anyway."

Another movement down the grand staircase caught Megan's eye, and she turned to see if Wade was coming back again. Much to her surprise, though, she saw Courtney walking down the steps, gliding along quietly but purposely. She moved quickly down the dozens of stairs, then made a beeline for the front door, and left.

Owen had noticed Megan's attention shift. "Courtney?" he said. "What was she doing upstairs?"

Megan returned her attention to the lean man. "Good question. You live in Rockport, don't you? Isn't that where she's living now?" All her focus on paperwork and time sheets was forgotten and her mind was tumbling with questions again.

"Yeah," said Owen. "A couple of blocks from me."

"Isn't everything in Rockport a couple of blocks from everything else in Rockport?" Megan said. Rockport was even smaller than Emerson Falls, with fewer than a dozen streets—and that's only if one was generous about what counted as a street. "What do you know about her?"

He shrugged. "Not a lot. She doesn't rub shoulders with locals much. People think she's very east coast."

Megan knew that "very east coast" was not necessarily a compliment around these parts. "Too good for her britches?" she said.

"Yeah, pretty much," Owen said. "Too good for us, anyway."

"Do you know where on the east coast she's from?" Megan asked. She remembered the conversation she'd had with Kevin. Had he mentioned a state, or just east coast? She couldn't recall.

Owen shrugged again. "East coast is east coast," he said. "It's that attitude. 'Where I came from is so much better than here, but never mind why I left.'" He clearly was not a fan. Megan wondered if maybe he'd suffered a rejection by an east coast love. Then she realized she had no idea about Owen's love life, or his life in general. Edison had been right about this building. With Owen downstairs and herself on the main floor, she hardly saw the man. That wasn't the kind of work environment she wanted to cultivate at all. As comfortable as she was, hiding away in her giant tree trunk, she knew she'd need to make an effort to reach out to all the staff and make them feel they were a part of everything. Megan wanted her staff to like working there.

"There's just something about her..." Megan said, returning her thoughts to Courtney. Then, she felt uncomfortable. Was she, too, judging someone simply for being from the east coast? Certainly she wasn't that petty. Was she?

"Well, no love lost here," said Owen, who clearly was not as interested in Courtney's presence. "Hey, I meant to ask, do you know who left the back door open downstairs? It was unlocked when I came in."

A shudder of unease whisked through Megan. She was sure she'd locked the door. Hadn't she? Reaching back in her mind, she tried to visualize her actions earlier that morning. When she'd let Edison in, she'd opened the door without unlocking it first. It had already been unlocked. Hadn't it? Had Edison somehow slipped the lock when she wasn't looking? On his way in or out? And why? The feeling she'd had earlier of trusting in him, in knowing he was safe, faded just a bit. Could it have been Wade, or Sylvie, or Baz? The fact was, none of them was careful about building security, and even she was still getting used to all the doors in this behemoth of a building. There could even be doors she'd not yet discovered. For all she knew, the door could have been unlocked for days. Owen didn't work Thursdays, so the door could have been unlocked since Wednesday when he left.

"I don't know, Owen. That's not good. I'll have a talk with everyone. Did anything look disturbed?"

"Just me" he said, and winked.

His unexpected sense of humor sometimes threw Megan off, but she smiled. "You are indeed disturbed," she said. "Well, sorry about that. We'll all be more careful. I'm most worried about the upstairs guests, about their not paying attention." She didn't say it, but Emlyn's cavalier, superior attitude was particularly bothersome. She could see Emlyn being quite careless about anything that didn't concern her. "I'll double check before I go to bed tonight. Thanks for letting me know."

Owen saluted and headed back downstairs. A few minutes later, Megan sensed a disturbance in the air around her again, and looked up once more.

This time it was Kevin who stood before her. "Kevin!" she said, a great smile bursting across her face. "What brings you here?"

He laughed. "Even I sometimes read," he said. "But I just needed to use the copier," he added, when Megan gave him a skeptical look. He waved some papers in the air.

"That sounds more like the truth," said Megan.

"Have you heard any more from Max?" he said. "Have they solved the case yet? Or have they gotten anything back from the coroner or whatever?"

Megan shook her head. "Nothing. He's keeping me at arm's length, I think. I'm trying not to take it personally." She smiled, and tried to remind herself not to be bothered by the fact.

"Okay. Gotta run," Kevin said, "but I thought I'd say hi while I was here. Didn't want you to think I was ignoring you. We still need to get a drink sometime again."

"Yes," said Megan. "Yes, we definitely do. Oh, hey—" she called out as he was rushing off, and he turned and came back. "Where on the east coast did you say Courtney is from?" she asked.

Kevin gave her a puzzled look. "Philadelphia," he said. "Why? What's up?"

Megan shook her head. "Nothing, I was just curious. I couldn't remember what you'd said. There seem to be so many people moving here from the east these days. I was just wondering."

Kevin's brow betrayed his confusion, but he didn't press the issue. "I gotta go," he said. "Give me a call." And he ran off.

As she watched him head toward the copier by the staircase, Megan was surprised to see Gus walking in the front door. He saw her and headed straight to her desk, a sheepish smile on his face.

"Hey," he said. He stood at the desk, somewhat awkwardly, and looked around the building. "Nice place you have here." He laughed weakly at his own joke.

"Hey, Gus!" Megan said, hoping her enthusiasm would encourage and comfort him. "Thanks. We like it. It used to be a mansion owned by Edison Finley Wright. Have you heard of him?"

Gus nodded, "Oh, yeah, of course. I'd heard that he owned the place. Hadn't been by yet. It's nice." He had his hands in his pockets, and was rocking back and forth on his feet, still taking in the grandeur of the space.

Megan could tell his mind was not fully on the architecture, though. "What can I do for you, Gus?" she said gently.

"So you're really a librarian, not with the press," he said, shaking his head a bit at another awkward joke. "I ... Well, I just wanted to come by and say thanks. For the talk. The other day. When Romy and I split up—" he paused. "When we split up, she got possession of all our friends. I became a bit of a hermit. I don't have a lot of people right now. I didn't really have anyone to talk to about Romy. You ... well, let's just say you came at the right time. I needed someone to listen, to ... to just be there." His eyes started to glisten and he looked up with fascination at the strings of lights overhead for several long seconds before looking back at Megan. "So, thanks."

"You're welcome," Megan said. She remembered after Zeus died, how everyone wanted to help but no one knew what to say. Because there was no right thing to say, as it turned out. She grabbed one of her business cards, wrote her cell number on the back, and handed it to him. "If you need an ear," she said.

Gus took the card and nodded his gratitude. "I will." He cleared his throat. "So this library! Mind if I look around? This whole thing was really a house once? Can you imagine?" he said, forcing cheerfulness into his voice.

Megan took the cue to move the conversation along. "Before it was converted, I had a chance to come in and look around. It was pretty amazing. But I think it would get lonely. Way too much space for one or two people. My apartment is upstairs," she nodded in the direction of the staircase, "and it's all I need."

Gus followed her gaze to the stairs, and looked up. "Behind that door, I assume?" he said. Megan nodded. "You get the whole upstairs to yourself?" He looked up and down the lower space again, seeming to calculate in his mind what the upstairs space must look like.

"No, no, not at all," Megan said, laughing. "There are some guest rooms upstairs, too. Romy's sister and brother-in-law are staying with me, and also Romy's agent. Well, her temporary agent. Emlyn. She's here, too."

"Emlyn," said Gus. "Yeah that's not her normal agent. What happened to Jordan? I liked Jordan."

"Jordan, that was her regular agent? Maternity leave, Romy told me. Busy populating the earth with more readers." She grinned.

"Huh," said Gus. He paused. "We never did that. Kids. I wanted to, but ..." He then seemed to get lost in the past, almost forgetting Megan was there. After a few moments, his eyes cleared and he returned to the present. He tapped his knuckles on Megan's desk. "Want to give me the grand tour?" he said, sweeping an arm wide to indicate the library.

Megan looked at the clock. Just before four. She'd been so preoccupied all week and was feeling quite behind in her work, but she knew what it meant to have human company when grieving. Straightening the papers on her desk, she stood. "How about the baby grand tour?" she said. "I have to get this done, but I can show you the highlights."

By the time Megan had showed Gus around the main level, with a quick run down to the conference area, most of the patrons had cleared out of the library. Friday nights were like that, Megan had noticed, and she made a mental note to think about whether they should close earlier on Fridays, maybe extending another, more popular, night, instead. Or, she then thought, maybe the people of Emerson Falls needed a reason to come to the library on Friday nights. She would have to think on it.

As they passed by the grand staircase on their way back to Megan's desk, she waved her hand toward the upstairs. "That, up there, is the living area, as discussed. And that's it, for now. Maybe more to come. We have a lot of space right now that we're just using for storage. And rooms that are just completely empty. I'm hoping we can find ways to utilize it all better."

Gus studied what he could see of the upstairs level, then looked out the great windows overlooking the river. "You must have a good view from up there," he said admiringly.

"I do," Megan said. She got the vague sense that Gus was going to ask to be invited up, but he didn't. Instead, he tapped the pocket in which he'd put her business card.

"Thanks again. Means a lot," he said. "I'll let you get back to work."

"Anytime," Megan said.

* * *

By the end of the day, Megan was itching to get outside. Once the library was shut down and all the patrons had gone home, she ran upstairs, changed quickly, and then headed out toward the falls. She took the same route she'd taken the other day for the fans' memorial. Amazing, she thought, how long ago that seemed now. It seemed that in the time between then and now, the seasons should have changed, the flowers in bloom should have withered, the water depth should have lowered. But there it all was once again, the reed canary grass, the Oregon grape. Addie Emerson's memorial park with its English yew and Scottish heather and tulips. Though it felt like it had been forever, time was standing still, waiting for justice for Romy's death.

As always, Megan felt as though the river itself were somehow connected to her own bloodstream, its coursing power helping to keep her alive. Of lakes, the ocean, and rivers, Megan liked rivers best. Lakes felt stagnant and enclosed. The ocean made her feel too small, which, admittedly, was good sometimes. But rivers felt infinite, like a Möbius strip, with no beginning and no end.

Waterfalls, on the other hand, Megan thought as she neared the falls and the roar started to fill her ears, waterfalls ruled over all the other forms of water. Having a home over the river was fantastic, but if she could one day have a cottage next to a secret waterfall with its own crystal clear pool? Well. Paradise.

She walked down the nature trail a ways and then veered off slightly onto a path that most didn't know about. Or if they did, they were careful, like she was, not to leave any trace of their passage. Where branches blocked her way she very gently moved them aside to let herself through, then eased them back into position. She walked on rocks when she could, trying not to leave footprints. Zeus had revealed this path to her on their third date. He had whispered in her ear that it was their secret, the puff of his breath tickling her skin and making her giggle. They must always take care to be sure they weren't followed, he'd said, as though they were spies on a secret mission. Most people were too lazy or reticent to strike out on their own, he'd said. "Or law abiding and careful not to disrupt nature," she'd teased, but she'd followed him anyway, feeling a special thrill at their escape from the beaten path. As long as possible, they would keep this place to themselves.

In reality, their secret waterfall was small, its drop only about five feet. The pool at its bottom was not much bigger than a hot tub. But it was theirs.

Until a year ago. A year ago it became hers alone.

Megan headed straight for her favorite formation of boulders, where one almost-flat rock served as a seat, and another acted as a backrest. She brushed a few pinecones and needles off the rocks, and sat.

"Okay, brain," she said as she let her eyes become mesmerized by the lull of the waterfall, "find the thing we're missing." She knew from experience that if she stared at the waterfall long enough, letting her thoughts flow as easily as the falls themselves, that ideas might start to pop up out of nowhere. Things that had been clouded would become clear. The obscure would become obvious.

Maybe.

She went over what she knew about the party, starting from the beginning. She'd arrived. She'd talked to Kevin. Romy had greeted her at the door and shown her the priceless Nancy Drew collection. She'd talked to Lily and eaten some of the perfect cakes Courtney had made, indistinguishable from the actual books. She'd met Emlyn and Baz. She'd watched Edison flirt with Romy. She'd had some wine. She'd gone home. Edison had stayed late. Sometime between when he left (so he said) and the next day, Romy had been drowned. Well, Megan thought, she wasn't sure about the logistics of the murder, but that part didn't matter. Max could deal with that. What Megan's brain needed to figure out was who did it.

"Courtney found her," Megan said out loud, just stating a fact rather than a revelation. Did that mean anything? Was that a cover? There was no gate around Romy's house. Anyone—absolutely anyone—could have gotten in. She believed Gus. She believed Edison. They'd ruled out that other author. But what about another writer? A jealous, bitter, aspiring novelist, some-one whose books were as yet unsuccessful? Surely a fruitless writing career would eventually take its toll. What's more, it seemed that Romy had played loose with the rules of story own-ership. If she'd taken liberties with Sylvie's life, and with Edison's, then it stood to reason she'd done the same with others, didn't it? For all she knew, if Romy had lived, Megan's conversations with Romy could have been woven into the next book. "And what about those big checks she wrote?" Megan asked the peaceful glen. She'd have to ask Max if he'd had any breakthroughs on that. Was Romy involved in something illegal? Drugs or ... or money laundering ... or ... Megan ran out of ideas.

A rustle of leaves brought Megan's senses to sudden alert. Black bears were not unheard of in this area, and with the re-cent wildfires destroying their natural foraging areas, they'd been ranging more widely than usual for food. She held herself still, ears perked, eyes watchful. For a few moments, there was no noise, and then she heard the rustling again. Then she saw it: a deer, staring back at her. Come to drink from the pond, Megan supposed, and she suddenly felt guilty for keeping the animal from quenching its thirst. Much as she tried, no new ideas were coming to her. What's more, the light was fading fast as night approached. She decided to head on home. "Drink up, little deer," she said as she passed where it had been, but it was already gone.

* * *

Back home, Megan soaked in her bathtub for a while, once again hoping to coax insights and inspiration from her mind. Once again, her mind refused to make any new connections.

But just as she was about to give in to the relaxation of the bubbles and the warm water, without fully knowing why, Megan sat up suddenly. Water splashed around her, some of it escaping over the edge. "What?" she said to herself. "What is it?"

Just one word came to mind: Courtney.

"Yes, I know, but what?" Megan said to the bathroom. Resigned to the knowledge that her luxurious bath was over whether she was ready or not, she climbed out of the tub, dried off, and slipped into her favorite flannel pajamas. It may have been April, but it had to be pretty warm before Megan would give up her favorite flannel pajamas.

She stood in her bedroom, trying to let whatever muse she'd heard before guide her again. "What now?" she said, but already her body was headed to her laptop. "Okay then," she said. "Google it is." She squinted hard, trying to remember Courtney's last name. Kevin had mentioned it at Rae's. She flicked her mind back to the pub. Kevin had been sitting next to her. What else could she remember? It was a four-letter last name, she was sure of it. Did it start with M? Moss? No, that wasn't it.

"Well, there's an easier way to do this," Megan said to herself. Into the Google search bar, she typed "Rosemary Grace Garrison Romy Courtney." Surely that would bring up something.

And it did. "Courtney Shaw, of course," Megan said, on seeing the search results. Now she could remember Kevin speaking the name, spelling it out for Max. This time she typed "Courtney Shaw" into the search bar. On a whim, she added "Philadelphia."

Unfortunately for Megan, the name was not completely unique. She sorted through various Courtney Shaws in Philadelphia, but none seemed to be the right one. She tried again, this time broadening her search: "Courtney Shaw Pennsylvania." When the long list of results came up, she clicked on "images," thinking that might be easier. She took a moment to conjure up a mental picture of Courtney: straight blonde hair, slender, polished, fake. Megan started as the word "fake" came into her mind. Where had that come from? But she decided to let the muse take over.

Browsing through the hundreds of photos quickly became tedious. Most were close-ups of individuals, which Megan could immediately dismiss. She zoomed in on a few group photos to look more closely at faces, but had no luck. Finally she came upon one picture that seemed to be of a group of sorority sisters. Megan again zoomed in on the photo, not expecting anything at this point, but her heart stopped for a moment when she realized she did recognize someone in the picture.

It wasn't Courtney.

It was Emlyn.

Megan's heart raced as she scanned the rest of the faces. Why did this picture show up in a search on Courtney's name? Was Courtney in the group, too?

And then she found her. Standing in the back, her face turned slightly, her gaze on another of the women. Her smile was smug, as though she had a secret. Whereas many of the young women were holding hands or had their arms wrapped around each other in sisterly love, Courtney stood alone.

thirteen

Megan had texted Max about Courtney and Emlyn being in the same old college sorority photo, but he hadn't replied. "As if there's something more important than an old college photo?" Megan had grumbled, and then she'd flopped into bed and fallen into a deep, dreamless sleep. She woke once in the night, when the light of the waning moon had broken through the trees and directly onto her eyelids. A glance at the clock, a turn in the bed, and she was asleep again.

Now it was morning, and Megan awoke feeling like she'd already forgotten something. Romy's memorial was to be held that afternoon at a tiny roadside church nearby. Romy had loved the church so much that she'd written a version of it into many of her books. The interior would only hold about six people, but this memorial was only for family and close friends anyway. Sylvie and Wade, Emlyn (although Megan suspected that was only a courtesy invite), Gus, Courtney, a few others. Rae had offered up the pub afterward as a gathering place for food and camaraderie, but Sylvie had declined. They'd all had enough of this place, it seemed, and they were ready to go home.

Having replaced the guests' towels and sheets the day before, Megan decided to go back and collect the dirty laundry to wash. It was Saturday, and the library was closed. Time to get caught up on chores.

She headed first to Sylvie and Wade's room. As she was about to knock, she felt herself tense up. Could she just leave a note instead? She hated to disturb them on this day of all days. But as she hesitated, the door opened, making her almost jump. She stood looking at Sylvie, who returned her look with surprise.

"Hello, Megan?" said Sylvie, making the greeting into a question.

"Good morning," said Megan, instantly thinking that of course the morning was not *good*, but it was too late to take back the words that had fallen out of her mouth. "Sorry. I thought I'd come by and collect the dirty towels and such. I hope it's not bad timing."

"No, no, that's all right," said Sylvie. She was already dressed for the memorial and made up flawlessly, as usual, put together in a way that made Megan think of the royal family. The way their clothes always were tailored perfectly, everything fit like a glove, nothing ever had a crease or a stain or a button loose. That was Sylvie. She would have fit in at the most exclusive of gatherings. And yet she had a gentleness about her, a softness, that made one feel welcome in her presence. Sylvie turned back into the room, disappeared briefly, and came back, arms loaded with sheets and towels. She transferred them awkwardly into Megan's arms, and both of them laughed lightly at the comedy of the exchange. "There you are," Sylvie said. "Thank you for this. I'm sure it's not in the normal job description for a Library Director."

"Oh, it's not a problem at all," said Megan. "I don't mind," she said, and she pondered the dozens of tiny little lies every person made every day. Little white lies, the lubricant of polite society. What would happen, really, if everyone started telling nothing but the truth, she wondered? Would everything fall apart? "I know the memorial is in a couple of hours," she said. "Is there anything you need today? Anything at all?" She found herself wishing she could spend more time with Sylvie. And now it was too late.

"I'm just off the phone with our lawyer. We have a few more details to see to tomorrow, and then we plan to leave on Monday," said Sylvie. "We're so grateful for your hospitality."

Megan wondered if Sylvie had cried over Romy. Not because she seemed cold, but rather because she seemed so calm and put-together. Behind closed doors, she imagined. Behind closed doors, all bets were off.

"If you're ever in Emerson Falls again," Megan said, "I hope you'll come by and say hello." She couldn't imagine what might bring Sylvie back, but then she realized there would be many estate details to be settled. The home, for example, would need to be emptied and sold. There it stood, not even finished, but yet soon it would be back up on the market. For a fleeting moment Megan wondered if she might like to live there herself, but the cost of the place—sure to be too high for her salary—and the fact that a woman had died there put an instant stop to those ideas.

"That's kind. Of course I will." Sylvie stood, patiently waiting, and Megan realized Sylvie was ready for her to leave.

"Be sure to say goodbye before you leave, then," Megan said, walking away. "And let me know if you need anything else."

"I will," Sylvie said. She stepped back into her room and closed the door.

Megan dumped the armful of laundry just inside her front door, and then headed on to Emlyn's room. She knocked lightly and waited, but Emlyn didn't come to the door. It wasn't early, but neither was it late: only about nine o'clock. Megan remembered Baz had gone out in the morning once on a run; was Emlyn a runner too? She knocked again, a little harder this time. "Emlyn?" she called out, but there was no answer. Megan decided to try again later. She headed back to her room, tossed Sylvie and Wade's laundry into the wash, and sat and read *Death of a Social Butterfly* until the wash cycle was done. About an hour later, she moved the wash from the washer to the dryer, and decided to try Emlyn's room again.

This time, she knocked loudly the first time, and then even louder another minute later. An hour had passed; surely Emlyn wouldn't be out running still? Or was she in charge of the memorial? Maybe she was out at the little church already? "Emlyn, are you there? I've come to get your sheets," she called through the door, deciding to knock one last time before she gave up.

Wade had heard the commotion she was making, and came out of his room, eyebrows raised. "Not there?" he said.

"Do you know if she's down at the church already? Setting up?" Megan asked.

"No, she's not," said Wade. "Courtney's in charge of everything. It's going to be a small ceremony, anyway. Not much to set up." He looked at Emlyn's door. "Do you think you should check on her?"

"I hate to be rude," Megan said. "What if she's in the shower?"

"You were knocking on her door about an hour ago," said Wade. "She can't still be in the shower."

Megan sighed. "Well, I'll give her another half hour," she said. "It's only, what, ten now? I'll try again about ten thirty."

When Megan came out of her apartment again just after ten thirty, Wade was there waiting. Megan looked at him curiously: why was he so interested in Emlyn's whereabouts? She headed down the hall and knocked again, loudly and firmly.

Again, no answer.

"I checked," Wade said. "Her car is downstairs. And she's not in the library."

A moment of shame rushed through Megan. Why hadn't she thought of those things? "That was smart," she said. "Thank you." She looked at the door, as if maybe, if she looked at it long enough, it would open itself. Finally, she reached into her pocket. "I brought an extra key," she said, showing it to Wade.

He nodded.

She raised her eyebrows in question to him.

He nodded again.

Megan slipped the key into the lock and felt the resistance, then a click as the door unlocked. She turned the doorknob and slowly opened the door.

Inside, on the floor, lying with her face turned in a pool of vomit, was Emlyn. Her lips were blue. Her eyes were open.

She was dead.

* * *

Twenty minutes later, the upstairs hall at the library was a frenzy of people. The EMTs had arrived and quickly confirmed what Megan had seen from the doorway. Max arrived shortly after the EMTs, and was now calling in for a forensics team. After he was done, he turned to Megan, who had been waiting in the hallway, not wanting to stay but unable to pull herself away.

"Poison, or something toxic, I'm guessing," he said, staring at the fluid on the floor. "Did you see or hear anything unusual or suspicious in the last twenty-four hours?" he asked.

"Twenty-four hours?" said Megan. "You think she's been dead that long?" The thought was nauseating. Imagining a dead person just feet away from her as she slept. She shuddered.

"I can't say yet. Probably not," he said, looking back at Emlyn's lifeless figure, "but I need to cover all bases."

"I was completely out last night," Megan said. "I mean, sleeping. Here. Out like a light. Hardly woke up at all. But this morning, well, Wade seemed awfully eager for me to check in on Emlyn. It was sort of strange." She thought back to earlier that morning. "He was hovering. He hovered. I didn't suspect anything at all yet, but he was out here, waiting for me to go into her room. When I came out the last time, he'd already checked to see if Emlyn's car was outside, and he'd looked for her in the library." Megan paused, thinking. "Or *had* he? I just assumed he was telling the truth. I didn't ask. I didn't check myself. Maybe he'd just wanted to hurry me along, to get me to look in on Emlyn, when he already knew what I'd find?" Megan gave Max a long look. "You should talk to him," she said. "And, I don't know, check for his fingerprints inside there. Or whatever you do."

"We will, for sure. Thanks for that." Max glanced back into the bedroom at Emlyn, a stern look on his face. "Something I didn't tell you," he said. "Those big checks Romy wrote recently, they were written out to a company that traces back to Emlyn and her husband."

Megan's mouth formed a silent *Ohhh*. "You're kidding!" she said. "Emlyn and her husband? But Baz has gone home already. Or at least, that's what Emlyn said. Maybe he's not actually gone but is actually dead?" She gasped, her eyes drifting to the large cedar chest in the bedroom. Could Emlyn have stuffed Baz into the chest? "Oh my gosh. Do you think Baz is dead?"

Max raised an eyebrow. "Don't panic just yet. I'll have someone check on that. It'll be easy enough to find out if he flew home."

Megan let out a breath. "Okay. Okay. So the checks that Romy wrote to Emlyn and Baz's company. How much were they for?" she asked.

"Several checks, several thousand each," Max said, but he

didn't elaborate. He nodded at the door. "You're saying this was locked when you tried it this morning?" he asked.

"Yes, and Wade can confirm that. One thing, though," she said. "I'm still getting used to this huge house, and having all these people around …" she paused.

"Yes?" Max encouraged.

"There have been unlocked doors. I've forgotten to check every night. Owen said when he came in yesterday afternoon that the door was unlocked downstairs. The bottom level, where the conference rooms are. I'd met with Edison in the morning, so maybe I forgot. But it's not the first time. This hallway door that opens to downstairs," she indicated the door by the stairs, "I've found it open a few times, too. Unlocked." Megan lowered her voice. Sylvie and Wade had come out earlier to see the commotion, but had since returned to their room, Sylvie looking very pale. "Sylvie goes downstairs at night sometimes. I'm sure her mind isn't on locks. I don't know if she always checks, and I don't know if she went down last night. Like I said, I was asleep. Dead to the world." She cringed at her choice of words.

Max went to the door. He and the EMT had come up the back way, through the living quarters entrance, rather than through the library and up the stairs. After putting on a pair of blue gloves that he pulled from one of the many pockets of his uniform, he tested the door. It was unlocked.

"Is the door unlocked during the day?" asked Max. "While the library is open? Could someone have gotten in?"

The memory of Courtney waltzing down the stairs rushed to Megan's mind. "Courtney," she said. "Courtney was there yesterday. Max, did you get my text? About Courtney and Emlyn?"

"I did," said Max. "Tell me more. You saw a sorority picture of them together?"

"Yes. I mean, I know that's not incriminating in and of itself. It seems weird that Emlyn didn't mention that she knew Courtney, but then she and I weren't close. And—" she paused again.

Max shook his head with a combination of amusement and impatience. "And?" he said. "Go on?"

"I've been thinking. I had this thought yesterday, before I even knew the checks were written out to Emlyn, and before I knew that Emlyn and Courtney have known each other a long time. You weren't at Romy's party, so you didn't see the cakes Courtney made. The art was perfect on them. Each one looked exactly like the covers of Romy's books. Like, *exactly*. Someone who can replicate a book cover that closely ..."

"... Might be able to forge a signature," Max said, nodding slowly.

"Exactly. That's exactly what I was thinking. What if Courtney wrote out those checks? What if she and Emlyn were ... conspiring? And maybe Romy found out so Courtney had to kill her, and now Emlyn's dead because she was a liability? Maybe if you look into Romy's accounts, I wonder if you'd find Courtney's been taking a little off the top the whole time she's been there? Romy didn't pay attention to that sort of thing, Gus told me. She might never have noticed. She was making money from her books hand over fist. If she trusted Courtney, she wouldn't have paid attention. And then with Emlyn taking over Romy's account temporarily, well, the time was right, wasn't it, to do something big? Except maybe it got out of hand—"

Max's sparkling smile was growing as the wheels started to turn in his head as well. "Megan, you may be on to something here. You may well be on to something. I'm going to get someone over to Courtney's right now." He turned away and got on his walkie-talkie to make the call.

Megan crept up to the edge of the doorway to look in one more time. Luckily, she thought, Emlyn's body hadn't begun to decompose and smell yet. She couldn't imagine how awful that smell would be and she didn't ever want to find out. Much less to be responsible for getting the stench out of the room. She shuddered.

She looked around the room to see if there were any more clues. The forensics team was sure to take away all evidence and shut the room down soon, so this was her only chance. What to look for, she wondered. The bed was unmade, but that was how it had been the other day. A mess all over, she remembered. Papers spread around everywhere, and the laptop … "Wait," Megan said out loud.

Done with his call, Max turned around. "Wait what?" he said.

"Papers. When I came by the other day … yesterday? Was it yesterday? Anyway, when I came by, the room was a mess. There were papers everywhere. All over the desk. And her laptop …." Megan looked around the room again, trying to peek around the door without touching anything. "Where's her laptop?" she said.

Max put his arm on Megan's back as he stepped gingerly around her, also avoiding disturbing any evidence. He scanned the room from the doorway. "I don't see one, either. I'll tell forensics to check for it," he said. "There were papers all over?"

"*All* over," Megan nodded. "And a giant stack of papers, with a huge red binder clip. I don't see that now." She got down on the floor outside the door, trying to see the room better from that angle without going inside. "Nothing under the bed, as far as I can see, but the comforter is hiding part of my view."

"What about that food?" Max said, pointing to the gift basket across the room on the table. "Do you know where that came from?"

A rush of warmth spread up Megan's neck. "Oh, that's from me. I put together gift baskets for Emlyn and for Sylvie and Wade, too. Lily—" She stopped.

Max raised his eyebrows.

Megan shook her head. "Lily brought some stuff for it too,

when I asked her to help me, but you know Lily. I'm a thousand percent certain that anything she brought was delicious, but not poisonous."

Max looked across at the basket. "I'm sure you're right," he said. "But we'd still better check." He sighed heavily. "And if you could stick around a bit, I'll need to ask you some questions."

His serious tone made Megan's blood run cold. "Me?" she said. "I mean, of course, I'll be around." Her mouth hung open for a few seconds, held by words that wanted to come out. But she kept them in. *You have the right to remain silent*, she told herself. She cleared her throat and studied Max's face to see if she could tell what he was thinking, but he'd put on a mask of detachment. Megan shivered. "Let me know when you're ready," she said.

As she walked back to her apartment, the door to Sylvia and Wade's room crept open, eventually revealing Wade standing there, looking down the hall toward Emlyn's room and Max. His face had gone pale. Behind him, Megan could see Sylvie lying on the bed, fully clothed, completely still, eyes closed, her breath measured and slow, her hands clasped across her stomach.

Wade brought his focus from the scene down the hall back to Megan. "Does he know anything?" he said.

Why did it seem like Wade knew something he hoped Max wouldn't find out? "Forensics is coming," Megan said. "He'll know more then. You might—" she looked back at Max. "I think Max will want to talk to all of us," she said. "I'm sure he won't mind if you go to the memorial, but you might want to check in with him. So he knows where you are. Where you'll be."

"We've decided to leave tomorrow," Wade said, a rush of blood putting the color back to his face.

Megan shrugged. "Just a suggestion," she said. "I have no authority here." She turned and went back into her home. Without really thinking about what she was doing, she headed to the kitchen, quickly brewed up some very strong coffee, then went and sat on her balcony.

She felt numb. Before Max had said he wanted to talk with her, she'd been full of adrenaline. Now, she felt numb. And nauseated. She drank in a sip of the brew, closing her eyes as the almost-too-hot liquid trickled down her throat.

Who could have done this? Who could have killed Emlyn? Had the same person killed both Emlyn and Romy? And why? Was it Wade? If so, what could he have had against his sister-in-law, and Emlyn? Were the murders connected, or was there someone in town, some psychopath lurking in the shadows, unnoticed and invisible, who was just targeting random women for his own sick pleasure? Instinctively, Megan looked back toward her front door. Had she locked it when she came in? She was the type who usually locked doors, but she was also the type who thought locking doors wasn't really necessary here in Emerson Falls. Megan stood and walked over to the railing. Holding tight, she craned her neck to look over the side. Could a person climb up from below? Up onto this balcony, or onto the one outside her bedroom? It wouldn't be easy, she decided. But it would be possible. What's more, the same isolation that let her sleep with the curtains open at night would give cover to anyone who might want to try their hand at scaling the wall. Someone could even drive in with a ladder and go unnoticed. And what about all the other doors and windows in this monstrosity of a house? Megan decided she would need to talk with Owen. For her own peace of mind, they were going to need to create a better security system. And maybe she'd talk to Edison about it, too.

That is, if he didn't turn out to be the killer.

Megan's phone vibrated in her pocket, startling her and making her almost spill her coffee. A text from Max: "Are you inside? I'm at your door."

Without texting back, she went to the front door and opened it to find Max standing there, looking even more grim. She steeled herself for the conversation they were about to have. *I'm innocent*, she reminded herself. *Just tell the truth.*

"I'm going to have to talk to you later," Max said. "Courtney's dead, too."

fourteen

Max rushed off without another word. Down the hallway, Emlyn's door was open and people in disposable white forensics suits were milling about, muttering quietly amongst themselves. Hesitating only a moment, Megan ambled slowly down the hall, trying to look nonchalant and innocent.

"Hi," she said to the first man she encountered. He was about her height, slim, with wire-rimmed glasses and a look of focus and concentration. "I'm the Library Director. Do you, uh, are you guys all good here?"

"We're fine, miss," he said, and walked away.

"Nothing?" A voice behind her made Megan jump. She turned and saw Wade, a slight smile on his face. "Sorry. Shouldn't have crept up like that."

Megan put her hand on her chest as though she could calm her heart that way. "Nothing yet," she said.

"Max came by," Wade said. "Asked us to stick around." He wasn't looking at Megan but past her, into Emlyn's room. Emlyn's body was being transferred into a thick black body bag.

Wade seemed transfixed by the spectacle, but Megan couldn't watch. She turned away.

"Did he say anything else?" Megan asked.

Wade turned his gaze to Megan. "He said Courtney is dead." He paused, seeming to watch for Megan's reaction.

"Yeah, he told me that, too," Megan said. "I suppose he wanted to see our faces when we found out." She was studying Wade's facial expressions as much as he was studying hers. "Oh come on," she said finally. "How can anyone suspect me? Who is Emlyn to me? What do I know?" she said.

"Of course they want to talk to you. It is your house, after all," Wade said, keeping his eyes on Megan in a way that was quickly becoming unnerving.

"But I didn't know her," Megan objected. "I didn't even know Romy, for that matter, hardly at all. What about you? How well did you know Emlyn?" she asked.

"Never met her before the housewarming," Wade insisted. "And neither had Sylvie."

Exhaustion suddenly washed over Megan, and she wanted nothing more than to get away from that house. The very air seemed stifling, and the nearness of a dead body was more than she could take. "I'm sorry. I have to go. Please be sure you lock the doors behind you," she said, and headed back to her apartment.

Just then, Sylvie opened the door to their room, and stepped out. She looked as if she'd aged ten years in the time Megan had known her.

"Wade," said Sylvie softly, "we need to be heading out soon." She walked back into her room and shut the door.

Megan's heart filled with compassion for this woman who had lost her sister and yet was carrying on with such grace. Surely such a woman wouldn't be married to a murderer. "You guys can stay here, of course, as long as you need," she said to Wade.

"If I can do anything …" she trailed off. There wasn't much that she could do, she knew. Clean sheets and towels couldn't go very far toward healing a broken heart.

Wade's face softened. "Thanks, Megan. You've been very kind. Sylvie enjoyed talking with you the other night. She appreciated that you listened."

Tears started to fill Megan's eyes, so she quickly looked away. "Of course. Anytime. You know where to find me."

Wade gently held Megan's shoulder for a moment, then turned to return to his wife.

Megan inhaled deeply; exhaled slowly and loudly.

"I need a burger," she said to the hallway. A man in a white disposable suit looked up. Megan waved, and returned to her home. She grabbed her purse and coat, and headed out the front door. Then she went back inside, checked that all the windows and balconies were locked, and headed out once again.

She walked down the hall, just to check that everyone had what they needed, or so she told herself. "Hi, I'm the Library Director, Megan Montaigne. Everything going okay?" she said to a short white-suited woman.

The woman gave her a patronizing smile. "We're fine, thank you. It'll be a few more hours. We'll want you to keep clear of the room for a while longer, though." She stepped aside to let another of her team walk by. He was carrying the gift basket Megan and Lily had put together, encased carefully in a sealed, large, clear plastic bag.

On seeing her effort at being a good hostess carried away as evidence, Megan felt her heart sink. What's more, she thought, it was such a waste of Lily's good cookies. She looked into the bag, not really focusing, but then something caught her eye. "Wait!" she said.

The man stopped. He looked at his colleague, who shrugged her shoulders.

"Yes?" the man said.

"Those biscuits," she said, pointing into the plastic bag. "Where did those come from? Were those in the basket? We didn't put those in there. Those aren't from Lily and me." She wracked her brain to remember everything Lily had brought. "I'm sure of it," she said. "Lily didn't make those, and I didn't put anything homemade in. Those look homemade."

The man straightened a bit. She'd caught his attention. "Which ones?" he said, holding out the basket.

"Those," Megan said, tapping on the outside of the bag. She leaned over and scrutinized the biscuits. They were small, and flecked with some herb. They looked delicious. But where had they come from? "Were they in the gift basket?" she repeated.

"I'm afraid we can't say anything yet, ma'am," said the short woman.

"But those aren't from us. We didn't put them in there. Those aren't from us." She felt herself starting to sweat. If Emlyn had been poisoned, could the poison have been delivered in a biscuit? "Tell Max those aren't from us."

"All right, ma'am," said the short woman, casting a meaningful glance at her colleague. "Are you headed out for a few hours?" She made her face open and bright, but Megan could tell she was fishing for information.

"I'm going to Rae's," Megan said. "Don't worry, I'm not leaving town." Heart in her throat and the feeling of blood rushing through her ears, she turned and walked away.

To help calm her nerves, Megan took a long detour on her way to Rae's, walking alongside the river on the trail to the waterfront memorial for poor Addie Emerson before heading back north to the pub. When she reached the memorial park, she decided to go in. Opening the gate, she gave silent thanks to the garden club that kept up this little space. Footprints drying in the mud told her others had visited recently. The space was appreciated by the community, and it was well used. The gate opened easily, and the bench, which she now went to sit on, was clean. The plants were neatly pruned and the grass had been recently cut. The quiet space felt like a sanctuary.

As Megan sat, she felt like every cell in her body was rushing as fast as the river. She tried to take deep breaths. Nothing to worry about, she told herself. Nothing to worry about. Max knows me. All is fine.

She looked at her phone to check the time: just before eleven. She quickly texted Lily to tell her she was headed to Rae's, and then texted Rae: "Are you at the pub? I am in desperate need of a Rae's burger and good company."

Thirty seconds later, Rae texted back: "Just got in. Heating up the grill. I've heard the news. Come on by."

A laugh escaped Megan's lips. Of course Rae had already heard. How the news got to her so fast, Megan had no idea, but it always did. By the time Megan got to Rae's, Rae would know more than Megan did, if she didn't already. Her energy restored by the prospect of having someone to confer with on the day's events, Megan hopped off the bench and quickly walked the rest of the way to the pub.

When she got there, the scent of a juicy burger greeted her at the door. "Hello!" she called into the dimly lit room. "I'm here!"

Rae poked her blonde-white head out of the kitchen. "Burger's almost ready. Sit down and I'll be out in two shakes." She disappeared back into the kitchen.

Megan sat at the bar and took off her coat. She noticed someone had carved the initials "L+C" into the edge of the countertop, and idly searched her brain to see if she knew what local L was in love with what C. Before she could come up with an answer, Rae brought out the much-anticipated burger and a heap of fries. She put it on the counter in front of Megan, and stole a fry off her plate.

"Okay," said Megan. "What have you heard?" She took a bite of the burger. "Oh, yes, Rae. No one but you. So good."

Rae shook her head. "Go on," she laughed, then her expression turned to a combination of seriousness and gossip. "Well, I've heard that agent is dead," she said. "And that assistant, too. Romy's assistant."

"Courtney. Are there any more details on her yet? That's pretty much all I know," said Megan. "Honestly, I'm a little freaked out. How did someone get into my house to kill Emlyn?" An involuntary shudder passed through her.

"Haven't heard much about Courtney," said Rae. "She lives over in Rockport. Police found her. That's about it."

Megan nodded and wiped the corner of her mouth with a napkin. "I was telling Max that I'd been searching online, and found out Courtney and Emlyn knew each other. Sorority sisters, from what I can tell. He sent someone over to ask her some questions."

"They were sorority sisters?" said Rae.

"Yeah. Well, maybe. They were in the same picture anyway. And when Max told me that some big checks were being written from Romy's account to Emlyn, it occurred to me that Courtney was in a perfect position to do so. She was a terrific artist. She could easily have forged that signature."

"Art and forging aren't the same thing," said Rae, looking out the window as someone passed by.

"No, but you could see that a person who could perfectly imitate a photo could also perfectly imitate a signature," Megan said.

"True," said Rae, eating another fry. "Were all the big checks to Emlyn? You'd think if Courtney was forging checks she'd write some to herself, too."

"I haven't heard either way. Things were a little crazy this morning. Max wants to question me."

"That's his job, honey. It doesn't mean anything."

"I know, but it's terrifying," said Megan.

"Well, you've got nothing to be scared of. Just tell the truth. He knows you. But he still has to do his job. When is he going to talk to you?" said Rae. Seeing a spot on the counter, she whisked a towel from the waist band of her apron and wiped it down. She then pulled out two glasses from behind the counter, and poured each of them a glass of water.

"Thanks," said Megan, taking a sip. "He was going to this morning, until he had to go off to Courtney's." She put her burger down, her stomach feeling too unsettled to eat any more. "Rae, you have to keep me updated. I don't know how you find things out but you always do. If you hear anything, call me. You have to let me know because Max thinks I'm a suspect and won't tell me anything."

Rae hesitated.

"Rae!" said Megan, her eyes rolling. "Don't be ridiculous. You know I wouldn't kill anyone. If you hear anything, call me."

The pub owner stood and indicated Megan should stand, too. Rae then pulled Megan in for a hug, surprising Megan. Hugs were not Rae's thing. But the hug was sincere and Megan sank into it and suddenly found herself starting to cry. She only let the tears flow for a few seconds before she stopped them: *everything will be fine. Everything will be okay.*

After many long moments, and feeling much calmer, Megan pulled away. "Thanks, Rae."

"I will call you if I hear anything," Rae said. "You are going to be fine." She looked at the half-eaten burger on the plate. "All my extra effort and you're leaving that behind? *That* they should put you in jail for."

Megan laughed. "Sorry." She felt a vibration in her pocket and pulled out her phone, thinking it must be Lily, but it was a text from Owen: "You around? Call me."

"Owen lives in Rockport," Megan said, holding up her phone for Rae to read. "He must have heard. I'm going to head over there. I can't stand to go back to the library right now." She grabbed her coat and purse and gave Rae another quick hug. "You'll call me if you hear anything, right?"

Rae nodded. "Of course I will. You hang in there. And you call me if you hear anything, too."

Megan laughed. "You'll know before I do! Okay. I'll talk to you soon." She double-checked her seat to make sure she'd left nothing behind, and ran out the door.

"Ugh!" Megan said, remembering that she'd left her car at home. "Dang it!" She called Owen, but he didn't pick up his phone so she left a message that she was on her way. She then jogged the short way back to the library, skipping the scenic route past the park. She got into her car without going inside the building, noting that the swarm of police cars was still there. Sylvie and Wade's car was gone; they must have already left for the memorial. The ambulance was gone, as well, and likely Emlyn's body along with it.

After checking her phone for Owen's address, Megan drove quickly to the nearby town of Rockport. When she got to Owen's house, he opened the front door before she could even get out of her car.

"Been waiting for me?" Megan said as she walked up the broken, moss-covered walkway.

Owen looked like he was about to burst. "You heard?" he said, standing aside so Megan could enter his house.

The home was immaculate, far cleaner than she expected, but then, she figured, it made sense that he would be a clean fanatic. The furniture was sparse but in good repair: a long black leather couch, two mismatched chairs, and a low glass-topped coffee table with nothing littering its sparkling top. But Megan didn't sit, and neither did Owen.

"I heard," Megan said breathlessly. "You heard about Emlyn?"

The look of surprise gave Megan her answer. "Emlyn? No, what happened?" Owen said.

"Dead," said Megan, thinking how cold and callous the word sounded. "This can't be a coincidence."

Owen dropped into one of the chairs. "You are kidding me," he said. "Where? How?"

"We found her in her room this morning. Owen, are you always sure to lock all the doors at the library when you leave? Like, do you have a system to remind you?"

At this, Owen's face turned slightly red. "No, honestly." He paused. "I guess in the back of my head I figure you live there so you'll check everything after we're all gone." He shook his head, angry with himself. "That was stupid. I mean, I lock up, yes, but I've never worried about it too much."

"Someone got in," said Megan, still standing. "Do you know where Courtney's house is?" she asked. "I want to talk to Max."

"Yeah," said Owen. "It's right around the corner. There are only a couple of streets in town. Hard not to know where someone lives."

"Can you take me there?" Megan said.

"Sure," said Owen. He grabbed his coat and led Megan out the door, careful to lock it behind him. "This is insane," he said.

They walked a few hundred feet and turned down another small road. Megan instantly knew which house was Courtney's by the gathering of police cars outside, slightly smaller than the number of cars at the library. There was no ambulance, so Megan assumed Courtney's body had already been taken away, as well.

Looking around, her eyes finally found Max, who was talking to a policewoman.

"Max!" Megan called out as she approached him, Owen following along behind her. A mixture of emotions crossed Max's face before he put on the professional mask again, and Megan felt disheartened. She reminded herself of what Rae said: he was just doing his job, and that was part of what she loved about him. He had integrity. He was fair. And he would be fair in this, as well. She just needed to trust him.

"Max," she said again, stopping and acknowledging the policewoman with a nod. The officer nodded back, exchanged a look with Max, and left. Megan continued. "You have to check for something in there." She looked toward Courtney's house. It was small but freshly painted, with a trim garden out front and a bright red front door that was propped open to let the forensics team move about freely.

"Megan. What do we need to check for?" said Max. Megan realized his expression was not unkind or indifferent, but it was definitely closed.

"When they were taking evidence out of Emlyn's room, they took the gift basket."

"I'm sorry, Megan. We have to."

"I know, I know," Megan said, waving her hand. "But I saw what was in the basket, and there was something in there that I hadn't put in it. There were these biscuits, like little savory biscuits, some sort of herb in them. I don't know what they were, but we didn't make them. I don't know if it matters, but maybe, if these murders are related …"

Max nodded. "Okay, thanks, Megan. I'll have the team check. Anything else?"

Megan swallowed. "Do they know yet what killed either of them? Did they have a guess?"

Max glanced up at the clouds. "They agree it was poison, probably," he said.

"Both of them?"

"Both of them."

Megan felt a surge of fear-laced adrenaline.

"I can't talk more right now, Megan," said Max, "but I'll come by this afternoon. Will you be at home?"

The idea of going back to the library was horrible, but she wasn't sure where else she would go. "I'll be there. Let me know when you're coming in case I'm out."

Max put his hand on Megan's shoulder and looked her in the eyes. "Thanks, Megan." His signature smile was missing, but the gesture felt somehow reassuring nonetheless. Max walked back to the police officer he'd been talking to earlier, leaving Megan and Owen behind.

"Biscuits?" said Owen. "You think they were killed by biscuits?"

Megan shook her head. "I don't know, Owen." She felt a buzz in her pocket again and looked at her phone. This time, it was Lily. "Rae filled me in," Lily had texted. "Where are you?"

"Over at Rockport," Megan texted back.

"Meet this afternoon?" Lily texted.

"Yes," Megan replied. "Will let you know when I'm home."

She turned to Owen. "I've got to go. If you hear anything, call me." She felt like that's all she'd been saying all day. *One of these days*, she thought, *I hope I get some answers.*

fifteen

When Megan arrived back at the library, the last of the police vehicles was just about to leave. The short woman she'd seen upstairs earlier stood by the car, writing on a small pad of paper. Megan parked, and walked over to her.

"Hi, again," Megan said. "All done inside?"

The woman looked Megan over before answering. "All done," she said. She tucked the pad of paper into one of her pockets. "Please don't go in the room until you hear from us."

"Okay," said Megan, starting to think about what kind of cleaning the room might need, and whether she would be able to convince the library board to let her hire someone to do it. Lily, maybe. Lily could handle that sort of thing. The messes she had had to clean up on occasion at her B&B were legendary.

The woman turned back to her car.

"Wait," said Megan, "I'm just wondering, do you know anything yet? What happened? Anything you can tell me?"

Over her shoulder, the woman said, "Nothing we can tell you, ma'am." She got into her car and left.

Standing and watching the car drive off to the main road, Megan noticed the library grounds seemed suddenly quiet. After only a week, she'd already adjusted to having more people around. Sylvie and Wade were still at the tiny roadside church saying their final goodbyes to Romy. Emlyn, well, Emlyn wouldn't be coming back, either. The police and forensics team were all gone now. The library was closed for the day. The sun was sparkling off the river; the water whispering and burbling as it raced by, telling its secrets to anyone who knew how to listen. In shadier areas of the lawn, dew still gleamed on the glass. An unseen bald eagle in the distance gave out its distinctive, sharp, high-pitched call. All around her, the world was calm.

Megan took a deep breath and exhaled.

* * *

Two hours later, Lily had joined Megan up on her balcony and the two were sipping tea while playing a game of cribbage. Lily had brought the game over to help Megan keep her mind off of everything. "Steve never plays cribbage with me," Lily said, after moving her peg once more, far ahead of Megan's. "Your shuffle."

"Because you always win," Megan said. She picked up all the cards and tapped them against her leg to straighten them before shuffling and dealing out the cards again. "So what's the latest with all the fans?" she said, frowning at the hand she'd dealt herself as she tried to decide which cards to lay away. With a resigned grimace, she picked two and turned them face down on the table between her and Lily.

Lily quickly picked her own two cards and lay them face down as well. "Most of them have gone home," she said. "Just one room still in use. A guy who is convinced Romy was trying to communicate to him through her books. He says she coded secret messages to him which, if read in the right order, revealed her true feelings." She lay a card on the table. "Four," she said.

"And those feelings were?" Megan said, playing a seven. "Eleven," she said.

"True love, of course," Lily said. She lay down a four. "Fifteen for two," she said, and moved her peg on the board.

"Of course," said Megan. She studied her hand. She was distracted and not paying attention and, she thought, just not in the mood. "Twenty-two," she said, laying down an eight.

"You mean twenty-three," said Lily, looking at her own hand. She lay down another eight. "Thirty-one for two, and a pair for two." She moved her peg again.

"So," Lily said. "Max came by my house. That's why I was later than planned."

Megan gasped lightly. "He did? To ask you about the gift basket?"

"Yeah," said Lily. "What I'd made, what I'd bought, when I'd bought it, where I bought it, what the recipes were, what you'd put in the basket, whether I'd seen you put anything in when you thought I wasn't looking, whether I was still there when you put the baskets out for the guests, on and on and on."

Megan absentmindedly ruffled the edges of the unplayed cards. "What did you tell him?" she said.

"The truth," said Lily. She shrugged. "I mean, what else could I tell him? The truth doesn't lead to you. I know that and you know that."

"Or you," said Megan.

Lily blinked. "No, I guess not. I suppose I didn't realize I was a suspect."

"You thought only I was?" said Megan.

"Well, it's just that I know I'm innocent. So I guess that's why I didn't think I'm a suspect."

"But you know I'm innocent, too, right?" Megan said, a slight edge to her voice.

"Of *course*," said Lily. "Of course I *know* that. I can't *prove* that. But of course I *know* that."

Megan said nothing, her mind in turmoil. They played a while longer before taking a break. Finally, Megan looked at the clock. "Four thirty." She gave Lily a meaningful gaze.

Lily laughed, knowing full well what that particular gaze meant. "I mean, it's five o'clock somewhere, and it's almost five here. I say yes. Bring out the wine." She followed Megan into the kitchen, where Megan chose a Riesling from the refrigerator.

"What time do you need to get back?" Megan asked, opening the bottle and pouring the bright liquid into two glasses.

Lily glanced up at the clock on the kitchen wall. "Well, maybe an hour. Steve knows all of this has been hard on you, and there's only that one crazy guest, anyway. I should be home by six, though. What time is Max coming by?"

Megan pushed the cork back into the bottle tightly and returned it to the refrigerator. "Honestly, I thought he'd be here by now. I wonder ..." She pulled her phone out of her pocket. "Argh, I missed his text. He'll be here at five." She looked at the clock again.

"Hmm," said Lily. "Well, he probably won't want me here while he talks with you. Good thing I walked over," she said, drinking her full glass of wine in one big gulp.

"Lily!" Megan laughed. "Good thing indeed! Want another glass? One for the road?" She reached for the refrigerator handle.

Lily wiped her mouth. "No, I'd better go so you have time to get ready. Call me when it's over. Just tell the truth. It'll all be fine." She pulled Megan in for a brief hug, then held her at arms' length and looked into her eyes. "You will be fine. Right?"

"Right, boss," said Megan. "I'll call you."

* * *

Max declined to interview Megan on the balcony, "As nice as it is out there, I'm sure." So instead, they were sitting at Megan's kitchen table. If Max was feeling as awkward as Megan was, he wasn't showing it.

"Everything coming along okay?" Megan asked. She wished he would open up and give her something, some clue, but clearly, things had changed since that morning.

"The team is great," said Max. "They're working hard."

"Any more news on Romy?" said Megan. "I was thinking, did Courtney write checks to herself, too? Or was it just Emlyn? You'd think that if she was writing checks—"

"Megan," Max interrupted. "I have to ask you some questions." He tapped on his tablet and looked up, his face revealing nothing.

"Okay," said Megan. She folded her hands in front of her, then hugged her arms to herself.

"Can you tell me about the gift baskets?" Max asked.

Megan tried to recall, down to the smallest detail. How she'd been trying to be a good hostess, and put something nice together since she'd sort of been neglecting everyone, and how she'd gone to the store and bought some items but the baskets had still seemed bare and empty, so she'd called Lily for help, and how Lily, of course, always came to the rescue.

"You didn't make anything homemade for the baskets? Or provide anything other than store-bought items?"

"No," said Megan.

"And Lily, what exactly did she include?"

"Well, there was potpourri—"

"I mean the homemade items."

"The potpourri was homemade."

"Just the food, then," said Max. "Homemade food."

"I think only the cookies," Megan said. "Those biscuits that were in the basket, we didn't—"

"What kind of cookies?" Max asked.

Megan wracked her brain for a minute before coming up with an answer. "Lemon rosemary shortbread," she said. "I'm pretty sure that's what she told me."

"And you're sure it was rosemary?" Max said.

Megan was taken aback. "I mean, that's what she told me," Megan said. "I didn't check. There was no reason not to believe her."

"So you didn't eat any of them?" Max asked.

A chill ran across the back of Megan's neck. She frowned. "No, why? I'm sure, I mean I don't—you can't..." She stopped. What was Max getting at? Lily? Certainly not.

"When did you last empty your garbage?" Max asked, looking toward the kitchen sink. "Is it under there?"

"Uh ... yes ... I guess Tuesday? Garbage day is Wednesday, so ..."

"So not since you made up the gift baskets?" Max asked.

"No, not since then," Megan said.

Max got up and went over to the kitchen sink. From his pocket, he pulled out a large bag and blue gloves. After putting the gloves on, he reached into the cabinet under Megan's sink, and pulled the garbage bag out of the trash can. Struggling a bit, he put the garbage bag into the bag he'd brought, and then sealed it up tight.

Megan felt as though she'd been drained of breath and blood. She couldn't make her tongue work to speak.

"Sorry, Megan," said Max, and it did look like he was truly sorry. He peeled off the gloves and, realizing there was now no trash can to throw them into, put them back in his pocket. Taking a deep breath, he looked Megan straight in the eyes. His gaze was not unkind, but it was firm. "Don't leave town, okay? We just need to get this all figured out."

Numbly, Megan gave the smallest shake to her head. "I'll be

here," she said quietly, and Max let himself out.

After he left, Megan poured herself another glass of the Riesling she'd been sharing with Lily, and took the bottle with her
out to the balcony. She sat staring at the water for a very long
time, glass in hand, forgetting to drink her wine.

A lively tune ringing on her phone startled her out of her
trance. It was Rae.

"Hello?" said Megan, feeling like her voice and thoughts were
coming through an endless tunnel, at the other end of which
things might start to make sense.

"Megan, it's Rae," said Rae. "I got news."

Instantly Megan's attention snapped back through the tunnel,
and she was hyper aware of Rae's voice on the other end.

"News? What news?" Megan said, almost holding her breath.

"You know I have a friend on the force," Rae said.

Megan didn't know that, but this was not the time for that
story. "Yes?" she said.

"They found out what killed Emlyn, and also Courtney." Her
pause was so long Megan would have slapped her if she'd been
in the room.

"What was it?" said Megan. "What killed them?"

"Taxine poisoning," Rae said.

"Taxine? What is that, is that like cyanide?" Megan said, nam-
ing one of the few poisons she could think of.

"No," said Rae, who was clearly relishing the act of delivering
the news. "Taxine is from the yew tree."

Megan was blinking, trying to absorb what Rae was saying.
"Yew? Pacific yew?" she said, thinking of the flat-needled coni-
fer that was common to the area.

"Possibly," said Rae, "but Pacific yew isn't that toxic, my friend
told me. More likely English yew, she told me. And you know
where there's English yew around here, don't you?"

Megan blinked again, as though blinking was her only method now of bringing information into her brain. "Addie," she said. "Addie Emerson's garden."

"Exactly," said Rae.

Rae rattled on a bit longer, but Megan heard almost none of it before finally Rae signed off.

All she could think about was Max's question.

You're sure it was rosemary?

sixteen

Megan couldn't shake the unsettled feeling the day had left in her. She wanted to talk to Lily, but couldn't bring herself to make the call. She wanted to go on a long walk to the falls, but the wind had picked up and the forecast was for heavy rain. Besides, it was almost seven o'clock, and the sun would set within the hour. To work off steam, she ran up and down the steps of the grand staircase until she was out of breath. Then she went into her apartment for a long soak in a bubble bath and then a dive into a good book before bed.

Sleep eluded her. She lay tossing and turning in bed for hours, listening as the wind blew and the rain tapped against the windows, watching as the shadows of the trees crept up and down the walls. Finally, she gave up and got out of bed to get a glass of water. When she passed the front door, a dim light seeping under the frame caught her attention. She knew Sylvie and Wade had returned earlier in the evening, but she hadn't had opportunity or, frankly, desire, to talk with them. Grabbing her phone and putting on a bathrobe and slippers, Megan then opened the front door and peered out.

Someone had turned on the overhead light in the hallway. Usually Megan left it off at night, but she imagined Sylvie and Wade must have been shaken by the day's events, too, and maybe the light was reassuring. Megan walked down the hall to the door that led to the public space. Unsurprisingly to her, she found it slightly ajar. She stepped through from the living quarters side to the library side, and, sure enough, saw a light emanating from the reading area.

Megan went back to her room, grabbed her keys, and locked the door behind her before heading downstairs. She walked softly so as not to disturb the quiet of the night but loudly enough that she wouldn't startle Sylvie.

Once again, Sylvie had ensconced herself in one of the cozy, welcoming, overstuffed chairs of the reading nook. The fireplace was glowing, casting flickering shadows around the rest of the room. Sylvie had turned on the reading light next to her, and was engrossed in a stack of papers. From the much larger stack next to her, it looked like she was just about finished with whatever she was reading.

"Hey," Megan said in something just above a whisper.

Sylvie looked up and gave a weary but warm smile. "Hey," she said.

"I couldn't sleep either," Megan said. She grabbed a blanket out of the ottoman and tossed a second one to Sylvie, then curled up in a chair and wrapped her blanket around herself. "How did it go today?" she asked.

Sylvie put down the papers in her hand. "It was okay. That church, it was really quaint. I can see why Romy wrote it into her books."

"Did anyone come and bug you?" Megan asked.

Sylvie shook her head ever so slightly. "There were a couple of people there, but they kept their distance. They were respectful, and kind."

"I'm so sorry," Megan said. "About everything. I just … I don't know what to say." She looked out the window. The rain was lashing against the enormous glass panes, and the trees were blowing wildly in the wind, sending shadows running and jumping in every direction. For a moment, Megan thought she saw something move outside, but then she decided it was just the storm.

Sylvie looked up in the direction of Emlyn's room. "Do they know anything yet?"

"Not yet," said Megan. "Not that they're telling me, anyway." She nodded at the stack of papers now sitting by Sylvie. "What are you reading?"

"Romy's last book. She'd just completed the first draft before we got here. I'm done, actually. Do you want to read it?"

"Sure," said Megan.

Sylvie gathered up the pages and tapped the edges into a clean stack, then reached onto the table next to her and picked up a binder clip to hold the pages together.

Megan almost cried out. The binder clip was bright red. Like the clip she'd seen in Emlyn's room. The clip and the papers that had been missing when Emlyn's body was found. How had Sylvie come by a stack of papers that belonged to a dead woman?

"Where did you get that?" she said, controlling her voice as best she could. In the dim of the room, with the shadows flashing about, Sylvie's face was hidden in half darkness.

"Emlyn gave it to me yesterday," Sylvie said. "She thought I might like to read it."

"She gave it to you yesterday?" Megan repeated. Was this the truth? Surely Sylvie wouldn't be flaunting the papers if she'd gone in and murdered Emlyn. On the other hand, she hadn't expected Megan to come down in the middle of the night. The reading area, long after hours, was normally quite secluded.

"Yes," Sylvie said. "I'm a quick reader. And it was a first draft. Romy's first drafts are—were—always shorter." She handed the pages over.

"What's it about?" Megan asked, taking the thick stack of papers.

"It's about a guy who dies in a plane crash, only it turns out it wasn't an accident," Sylvie said.

A sudden gust from outside slapped the bushes against the windows, and Megan felt the chill in her soul.

"A guy who dies in a plane crash?" Megan said. Her chest was tightening and her head was swimming.

"Oh gosh," said Sylvie, seeing Megan's face. "I spoiled the ending. I'm sorry. I wasn't thinking. It's still a good book, though. When you're done, can you give it back to me? That's the only copy, apparently. Well, unless they find Emlyn's computer. Romy's computer got a virus and it wiped out everything."

Megan swallowed hard. "Of course. I will."

The rain pounded against the window again and a bolt of lightning lit up the room, followed by another a millisecond later. "Wow," said Sylvie. "Quite a storm out there."

Unsure whether she could trust her legs, Megan stood, the manuscript feeling like it was alive and burning in her hand. "I'm going to head up. I'll see you tomorrow."

"Goodnight," said Sylvie, making no move to leave herself. "I'm going to stay here a while. Thank you again for everything. You've been so kind to us."

Megan nodded in response, then headed upstairs. "A coincidence," she whispered to herself as she headed down the hallway to her apartment. "Just a coincidence." She remembered suddenly a funny look Romy had gotten on her face when she'd told her how Zeus had died. Megan had dismissed it at the time. But now, the look took on new meaning.

Back in her bedroom, Megan turned on her bedside lamp, propped up her pillows on the bed to serve as a backrest, climbed under the covers, and started reading. The storm raged outside, lightning followed a few seconds later by thunder that crashed and shook the sky. The book started with the description of a man in a plane in free fall. By the third page, he was dead.

As Megan read through the manuscript, skipping past passages and skimming others in her quest to get through it faster, she found herself shaking. Some of the details were different, the personalities were different, the setting was different, but of one thing she was certain: she was reading Zeus's story.

Except the ending was different, too. In Romy's book, what investigators had ruled an accident turned out to be involuntary manslaughter.

It was three o'clock in the morning when she turned the last page. The storm had subsided, with the exception of an occasional gust of wind. The moon was starting to peek out from behind the dark clouds that were swiftly being blown away. Megan assumed Max would be asleep, but she sent him a text anyway, telling him how she'd come about the manuscript and what she'd just read, her fingers trembling as she tapped in her message.

The room suddenly felt close and tight, and Megan felt she was suffocating under the weight of Romy's words. She pushed off her covers, walked to the balcony, and opened the door. The air smelled of rain and wet earth and broken branches. Moonlight sparkled on the wet ground. Megan leaned over the railing to see if she could assess the damage the storm had done, but it was too dark to see much more than a few shadows that might have been tree limbs.

That's when she saw the ladder.

Megan screamed. A quick, loud scream that penetrated the night and then was quickly absorbed by the darkness, as though it had never existed.

The metal ladder was leaning up against the railing at the far end of her balcony. Jolts of fear like lightning shot through Megan's body. Without thinking, she rushed over to the ladder and with all her might pushed it away from the railing. It moved easily; she could tell no one was holding it or standing on it in the dark. Her heart pounded in her chest as she raced inside and bolted the balcony door behind her. Frantic, she almost ripped the curtains off their track as she pulled them closed. Megan looked around the room. "What do I do, what do I do, what do I do?" she murmured out loud as she stood, frozen in place. Move the bed in front of the window? Race to her car and drive away?

She felt nauseated with terror. She grabbed her phone and called Max, but he didn't answer. "Think, Megan, think," she said out loud. Maybe the ladder had been left by … a gardener? But she knew that wasn't the case. She couldn't decide if it was safer to stay or to leave.

Shouts in the hallway outside her front door made Megan's heart race so fast and hard she felt it would beat itself up through her throat. She walked as quietly as she could to the front door and put her ear up against the cool wood. *Whose voices*, she asked herself, but she already knew.

One voice was Wade's.

And the other was Kevin's.

Then the voices stopped, and all she heard was loud grunts and the sound of bodies hitting the walls and the floor.

I have to help Wade, Megan thought. She took a deep breath and opened the door.

Kevin and Wade were tangled in a whirling knot on the floor,

arms and legs flying as each fought for survival. Without thinking, Megan reached inside her door for the first thing she could
grab—a small but solid oak table that stood by the door, where
she tossed her keys and purse when she came home. She raised
it as high over her head as she could, and then screamed as she
brought it down hard, aiming for Kevin and hoping for luck.

The table hit its mark, but Kevin was full of rage and adrenaline and was hardly fazed. He turned on Megan, his eyes blood-
shot and crazy. Megan hardly recognized this madman as the
river rafter she'd once known. "Do you have it?" he yelled as
he got up and tried to run to attack her. But Wade was too fast,
reaching out from where he lay on the floor to grab Kevin's legs.
Kevin fell hard, his face smacking against the doorframe on the
way.

The silence was sudden and unnerving. "Is he conscious?"
Megan said, more to herself than to Wade, who was struggling
to sit up. "Are you okay?" Megan said, looking at her guest. He
looked dazed but lucid. His navy blue pajamas were rumpled,
and a button was missing. Blood trickled lightly from some
scratches on his face, and undoubtedly bruises would bloom
soon, but he seemed to have made it through the scuffle far better than Kevin had.

"What the hell just happened?" Wade said quietly, rubbing his
hand gently on his cheek.

The door to Sylvie and Wade's room opened. "I've called 911,"
Sylvie said. She went over to Wade and cradled him in her arms,
completely unconcerned about getting blood on her bathrobe.

Megan looked at Kevin. He might be unconscious now, but
she wasn't leaving anything to chance. "What can I tie him up
with?" she said, wracking her brain, which seemed to have
stopped working. An idea popped into her head, and she ran
to the kitchen, returning with a fresh roll of plastic cling wrap.
She went at it, wrapping the plastic around his wrists behind his

back and around his feet, going around everything again and again as tight as she could until the roll was used up.

The sound of approaching sirens cut through the night as Wade, Sylvie, and Megan all looked at each other in disbelief. "I'll go let them in," said Wade, wincing as he tried to get up.

"No, you stay here," said Megan. "I'll go." She picked up the oak table and handed it to Sylvie. "If he wakes up. Unless you have a better idea."

She wasn't sure whether the authorities would know to come around the back, but if Max was with them, he would know, she thought. Impatiently she waited for the elevator to take her down to the living quarters entrance, and sure enough, Max was there with two other police officers as backup. She let them in and gave a brief run down on what had happened as the elevator took them back upstairs.

"Kevin?" Max said. "Why?"

"I'll explain everything once we're upstairs. Sylvie needs to hear this, too."

When they got back to the scene of the struggle, Kevin was awake again and struggling against his bonds. Max took one look, and turned to Megan. His signature smile with his gleaming teeth that practically sparkled in the light of the hall had returned. "Cling wrap?" he said, amused.

"What can I say," Megan said, returning the familiar smile with a rush of relief. "I didn't have handcuffs."

* * *

The other officers took Kevin away. Megan filled in Max, Sylvie, and Wade on everything that had happened, outlining how she knew Kevin was the murderer of all three victims. And then they all parted ways and she fell onto her bed and went straight to sleep without even getting under the covers.

When she awoke it was nearly noon, and her phone was loaded up with missed calls, emails, and texts. The Emerson Falls grapevine was hard at work.

Megan texted back to Rae, Lily, and Owen, adding Max to the group for good measure: "Meet me at one thirty at Rae's. I'll tell you everything then."

She showered and dressed quickly. When she got to the front door she found the casualties of the previous night's struggles. The oak table had seemed fine the night before, but now she could see that one leg had been cracked in the fight. No one had taken the time to pick up the cling wrap, so she quickly scooped it up and threw it away. She grabbed her keys and locked her door, thinking this was the first time she'd felt safe in days.

The weather forecast was for rain again later in the afternoon, but Megan craved the fresh air. Once again, she took the long detour along the river before heading up to Rae's. When she passed Addie's memorial park, she stopped. "English yew," she said to the bush. "Who knew?" She then laughed. "I'm a poet and I don't know it." She turned and walked briskly the rest of the way to the pub.

When she arrived, just before one thirty, the others were all already there sitting at a table. Rae came in at the same time Megan did, and set a burger in front of an empty seat.

"On the house for our newest detective," Rae said, winking. She took a quick look around at the other patrons to make sure no one needed anything, and pulled up a chair for herself.

Megan settled down in front of the burger, realizing she hadn't eaten yet all day. The others had already half-devoured their own, so she dug in.

"Well?" said Lily. "Talk! Max won't tell us anything!"

Max smiled, his teeth twinkling in the reflection of the overhead lights. "I'm a professional," he said. "What can I say?"

"Well, I'm not," said Megan. She took a deep breath and let it out. "I'm so glad that's all over."

"I have so many questions, I don't know where to start. How did you know it was Kevin?" said Owen.

"It was that manuscript Sylvie gave me," Megan said. "Romy's last book, a first draft. Emlyn had given it to Sylvie and I saw Sylvie just as she was finishing it last night. Sylvie told me it was about a man who had died in a plane crash, but it turned out the crash wasn't an accident." She paused a moment as a wave of grief swept over her, so strong it felt it might wash her away. This reopening of the old wound: she knew she was going to have to deal with this later. She blinked hard to shut off those thoughts until she had time to sort through them.

"It probably wouldn't have struck me, except that people have been talking all week about how Romy was a great listener—but then would turn around and write their lives into books. Sylvie, Gus, Edison, they all had stories about how their conversations or situations ended up in Romy's mysteries. Even that other author who came to the library right after Romy was killed— Kurt? Kirk?—even he had said she had stolen his ideas. So it just seemed like a strange coincidence. I mean, I know I was reading a lot into it. Coincidences happen all the time. But she gave me the manuscript and as I was reading it, I knew. This was Zeus's story."

"But Zeus's *was* an accident, wasn't it?" said Lily, a sad look on her face showing she knew what answer was coming.

"We thought so," said Megan. "But I think we'll have to look into that again. In the book, there was the guy who died in the crash, and there was his friend, who owned the plane and let him fly it. Apparently there's some sort of device that detects carbon monoxide. It's not a built-in part of the plane. In the book, it's just a little device called a 'dead stop' that you stick to the dash of the plane. If it goes dark, you know there's carbon monoxide. It needs to be changed out every ninety days. And

in the book, anyway, the guy who owned the plane had neglect-
ed to replace it. And as a result, his friend flew the plane, not
knowing there was a carbon monoxide leak. He fell asleep from
the carbon monoxide, and he crashed."

She blanched, feeling nauseated again. *Don't think about it
right now*, she told herself. *Later.*

"So the plane Zeus died in was Kevin's?" Owen said.

Megan shook her head. "No, but Kevin worked at the hangar,
and he was in charge of maintenance of some of the planes. The
plane Zeus flew was one that Kevin had hoped to buy one day.
Its owner had lots of other planes and basically considered that
one Kevin's. He flew it all the time."

"But even if that's what happened, it was still an accident.
Wasn't it?" asked Owen.

Megan looked at Max. "I guess that's what the police and the
lawyers are going to have to figure out. As I understand it, involuntary manslaughter is, by definition, unintentional. But what
matters is, he never said anything. And he felt guilty about it.
And one day, he told Courtney the whole story."

"Courtney was his girlfriend," said Owen.

"Courtney was his girlfriend," confirmed Megan. "Now, I'm
speculating here but it seems that what happened next was that
Courtney told Romy at some point. Maybe they were chatting
one afternoon and got talking, and Romy, I mean, she drew stories out of you like she was spinning wool." She shook her head.
"So Courtney told Romy, and Romy wrote it into her next book.
Kevin found out and got scared. He killed Romy. Then he put a
virus on Romy's computer, and killed Courtney and Emlyn to
silence them."

"Why did they have to be silenced?" asked Lily.

"They're the ones who knew," said Megan. "Emlyn had a copy
of the manuscript, and she also had it on her computer. That's
why her laptop disappeared from her room. Kevin must have

come up to get it. He was there in the library that day, and I didn't even think anything of it. It was such a busy day. I saw Courtney coming down from upstairs, and I suspected her, but it never occurred to me that Kevin might be up to no good."

"But how did he kill Courtney and Emlyn?" Owen asked. "Romy was drowned, but they were poisoned, weren't they?" He looked to Rae, who nodded.

"Lily and I put together gift baskets for everyone staying in the library rooms. Just little things, soaps, tea, that kind of stuff. And Lily put in homemade lemon rosemary shortbread cookies." She looked at Max. "You scared the bejeezus out of me when you tried to make me think Lily had poisoned them with her cookies!"

Max smiled broadly. "I did not try to make you think that. I was just doing my job."

Megan shook her head indulgently. "Anyway. When the forensics team were taking the baskets out, I saw some biscuits in them that we hadn't made. I remember noticing they had flecks of some sort of herb. I'm guessing now that they were baked with bits of English yew in them."

"Does Kevin have an English yew plant?" said Lily.

"Does Kevin bake?" said Owen.

"He may not bake regularly, but anyone can make biscuits," said Megan. "And I don't know if he had an English yew tree, but there's one in Addie Emerson's memorial park. To celebrate the English part of her English–Scottish–Dutch heritage."

"Ohhh," said Lily. "Hmm. Is it that poisonous? How have we not had more poisonings?"

"I'm guessing the fence kept out some of the wildlife that might have otherwise eaten it," said Megan, "and most humans who go in there aren't eating it. Or using it on each other."

"Good point," said Lily.

"Okay," said Owen. "So Kevin gave the biscuits to Emlyn?

Why would she eat them? Did she know him?"

"She knew Courtney," Megan said. "They were sorority sisters. Courtney probably introduced them at the party. Emlyn would have had no reason to suspect that Kevin would hurt either of them."

"Do you think he meant to kill Courtney?" asked Lily. "Was that just an accident? I mean, she was his girlfriend."

"People kill their significant others all the time," said Max somberly.

"So how did I do, Max?" Megan said, looking at the deputy with a grin. "Did I get it all right?"

Max's response was to mimic locking his lips and throwing away the key.

Rae bust out a guffaw. "You tease." She looked at Megan. "Just before you got here, my friend on the force called. Kevin confessed. I think you got it pretty much right."

Max rolled his eyes. "Your friend on the force should not be telling you so much!" But nonetheless, he was still smiling.

Rae simply shrugged and smiled.

"But wait," said Owen. "The big checks. So Courtney didn't kill Romy because she was embezzling money from her?"

Megan looked at Max, watching for a reaction. "My guess is that Courtney was embezzling money, and maybe lots of it, and maybe passing it along to more than one person, herself included. I remember thinking how nice her house and clothes were, and I don't imagine Romy could have been paying her as much as all that upkeep would have taken. Still, I think that was just a coincidence. Am I right, Max?"

Max winked. "I can neither confirm nor deny," he nodded.

"Well," said Rae, "this calls for a celebration. Drinks are on me."

"It's five o'clock somewhere!" said Lily.

Rae went to get beers for everyone. Max leaned over to Megan and handed her a paper bag.

Megan raised one eyebrow at him. "What's this?" she said as she opened the bag. Inside was a pair of pink fuzzy handcuffs. She pulled them out, laughing. "Where on earth did you find these on such short notice?" she asked suspiciously.

"What can I say? I didn't have any cling wrap," he said with a wink.

seventeen

Lily, Owen, and Rae continued talking, recounting the details of the scandal, the excitement of catching a murderer making them almost breathless. Max indulged with a smile, occasionally relenting and tossing in a tidbit or fact. They put aside, for now, the fact that the murderer was someone they knew, one of their own.

It had been exhilarating, really, Megan thought, in a way. Catching Romy's murderer.

What she hadn't expected was that she would also open up an investigation about Zeus.

She needed to talk to Kevin. *This is what it feels like to need closure*, she thought.

Megan leaned over to Max and asked him quietly, "Where is he right now?"

Max's eyebrows popped up. "Kevin?" he said, keeping his voice low to match Megan's. The others didn't notice.

Megan nodded.

"You want to go see him?" Max said, a line of concern crossing his brow.

Megan nodded slowly. She saw Lily look at her out of the corner of her eye; aware of the situation, but giving Megan space. There would be many long talks with Lily after this, Megan knew. Many boxes of tissue and many bottles of wine. And many hours at her secret spot at the waterfalls, waiting for a peace that would be long in coming.

"You're sure that's a good idea?" Max asked. "Maybe wait a while?"

Megan drew a deep breath and shook her head.

Max studied her, looking deep into Megan's eyes in a way that felt almost invasive. Finally, he relented. "He's at the county jail." He paused. "Do you want me to go with you?"

Megan shook her head. "I need to talk to him alone."

"He doesn't have to talk to you, you know," Max said, his eyes still searching Megan's. "If he doesn't want to."

"I need to try," Megan said. She slipped out of Rae's without saying anything, leaving Max to explain to the others.

When Megan arrived at the jail forty-five minutes later, she learned that Max had called ahead. "Normally we wouldn't let you in," said the clerk, "but Deputy Coleman called and vouched for you. I'll see if Kevin wants to come out. Fill this out," she said, handing Megan a visitation form, and then she disappeared into a back office for a few minutes.

Fifteen minutes later, Megan had relinquished her purse and keys and was waiting for Kevin. She sat at a long, stark metal table, separated from the other side with thick plexiglass above the table, and metal below. The table was partitioned into several small cubicles along its length, with matching phones on each side within each cubicle. No one else was there.

A door opened on the other side, and a chill went through

Megan as she saw Kevin walking into the room in his orange jail jumpsuit. She had half expected him to be in handcuffs, but his hands and feet were free.

Seeing her, Kevin sat in the seat opposite her.

Suddenly, she regretted coming here. She wasn't ready. She didn't know what she wanted to ask. She didn't know what answers she needed.

They sat, silent, for a few minutes. Finally, Kevin picked up his phone. Gingerly, Megan did the same with the phone on her side, and held it to her ear.

"I'm sorry, Megan," he said. His voice was echoey in the receiver, though he was just a few feet away from her.

Megan felt a tingling in her neck as the tears threatened her eyes. She willed herself not to cry. Not yet.

"Why?" was all she managed to say before her emotions choked her words.

Kevin ran a hand through his buzz cut. "I just … I got scared."

"You were negligent in Zeus's death. But you could have come forward. You didn't have to do … all this." Megan said, pushing the tears back again. She inhaled slowly. *You're here, Megan*, she said to herself. *What do you need to know?* She realized she wasn't ready to talk much about Zeus yet. That could come later. But Romy. What had happened? "Why Romy?" she said.

Kevin shook his head and ran his hand through his hair. "I freaked out. After the party, Courtney, Romy, and I were sitting in Romy's living room. Romy started telling Courtney about how she'd been talking with you and you'd told her how Zeus died, and it sounded so much like the story Courtney had told her a year ago. She said her latest book was inspired by that story, and what a funny coincidence that was." He rubbed his hand on his neck. "Courtney never told me she'd said anything to anyone. I told her about the dead stop because I was scared.

I didn't think she'd tell anyone. But it turns out she told Romy about it right away. Didn't name names. Just laid it out like an interesting story. Romy took it and ran." He cradled the phone against his neck and started rubbing his hands together, rhythmically turning his left thumb over his right thumb, right thumb over left. "I got scared. She was going to publish that book and everyone would know. I drove Courtney home, then went back to Romy's. I'd only meant to talk to her, beg her not to publish the book, but ..." He turned his gaze to the high windows on the wall behind Megan, the sun filtering in like a verdict.

"You drowned her," Megan said.

"Yeah," Kevin said. "Just ... held her down. She was drunk. She wasn't that strong."

It was such a thoughtless thing to say. Megan suddenly felt the rage rising inside her, but she pushed it back down.

"Emlyn?" she said. "Why Emlyn? How?"

He shrugged. "She had the printout. I'd slipped in and put a virus on Romy's computer the next morning, before Courtney found her, but I didn't know Emlyn had the manuscript. I knew that yew in the park was deadly. I got some, baked some biscuits. I took them up to her and she didn't question it. Just ... ate them."

"And Courtney?" said Megan.

He seemed to shrivel into half the man he'd once been, slumping in his chair. "She knew everything," he said. He watched his thumbs, passing one over the other, like there was nothing else in the world to watch.

Maybe, thought Megan, he would have nothing to do but twiddle his thumbs for a very long while.

"The ladder? My balcony?" she said.

"I saw Romy's sister give you the manuscript," he said. "But your deck door was locked."

Megan felt a rush of gratitude that she'd remembered to lock the balcony door, at least that once. "So how did you get in?" she said.

"Downstairs," he said. "Through the garage," he said. "I unlocked it earlier in the day, when I took the biscuits to Emlyn. You took that guy on a tour of the place and didn't even notice me. After that, it was easy."

Exhaustion swept over Megan. She had nothing more to say. Without saying goodbye, she stood, hung up the phone, and left.

* * *

When Megan got back to the library, Sylvie and Wade were loading up their rental car.

"Oh, I'm so glad we saw you before we left," Sylvie said. "Can you send me Romy's manuscript once the police are done with it?" Max had told them that the police had to keep it, for the time being, as evidence.

"Of course," said Megan. "I'm so sorry for everything you've gone through. This all must be unbearable."

Sylvie reached out and put a hand on Megan's forearm. "Max told me about your fiancé. His plane crash. I'm sorry for you, too. Kevin hurt a lot of people here."

A sting of sadness came to the back of Megan's throat and to her eyes. *Not yet!* she told herself. "He did. But even so, I hope you'll come back again," she said.

"We need to take care of lots of loose ends," said Sylvie. "You'll see us again."

Wade slammed the trunk of the car. "Hopefully it'll be less eventful next time," he said.

Megan could see bruises at his neck, above the collar of his shirt, and one on the right side of his face. She winced. "I hope you heal quickly," she said.

Wade held out his hand. "I'll be okay. Thanks for coming out to save me last night," he laughed. "You should have seen the look in your eyes with that table in your hands. You're a bit of a warrior, I'd say."

Megan waved off his hand and pulled him in for a light hug, wary of his bruises. "Take care, Wade," she said. She turned and gave Sylvie a hug as well.

"We left you something," Sylvie said. "Inside our room. We wanted to wait to give it to you, ourselves, but … it's time to go."

As they drove away, Megan saw another car headed down the long driveway to the library. The driver pulled up slowly alongside Megan, and parked.

"Hey, Edison," said Megan as the library benefactor climbed out of the car.

"Hey, yourself, detective." He looked her up and down. "You look beat."

Megan laughed. "Thanks. I am beat."

"I should think so," said Edison. "I heard all about it."

Megan shook her head. "Word travels fast. So what can I do for you today?" she said. She started walking around back to the living quarters entrance, and Edison followed.

"I figured we should talk about what you need to feel safe here," Edison said. "Not just a new washer and dryer for the guests. But maybe," he looked up at what had once been his house. "Maybe if we're going to expect you to live here, and put up guests, maybe we should put in a little more security for you. Or at least talk about it. I came to look the library over and see what needs to be done."

"Can the library afford that?" Megan said. She knew funds were tight.

"It's on me," said Edison. "I want you always to feel safe."

She looked him over. She'd never really thought of him as a

peer, somehow. Always she'd seen Edison Finley Wright as a member of some local aristocracy. Someone who would never run in the same circles as the likes of Megan Montaigne. But after all she'd been through, after all she'd learned, she found herself wanting to get to know this person more. "Thank you, Edison," she said. "Thank you."

They headed up the elevator, and Edison went off to scrutinize the building while Megan went back to her home. She walked out on the balcony and sat for a while, staring at nothing, watching the river go by.

Suddenly, overhead, she heard the high-pitched chirp of a bald eagle. She looked up. A lone eagle was floating on the wind currents, high in the sky, flying in wide circles directly over the library. Megan watched as it stayed for many long minutes, soaring in circles ever farther away, until finally it was out of sight.

"I won't forget you," she said to the eagle as it disappeared.

* * *

After a while, Edison left with promises to return soon. Shortly after that, Megan felt her phone buzzing in her pocket. A text from a number she didn't recognize. "This is Gus," the text began. "I've heard the news. I'm sorry. This has to be devastating. If you need to talk, I can listen."

Megan smiled and put her phone away without replying.

She'd just started thinking about the prospect of cleaning up Sylvie and Wade's room, when she remembered that Sylvie had told her they'd left something for her. Curiosity building, she headed into their room.

They'd left the room very tidy, of course, and the bed was made to hospital perfection. On it lay dozens and dozens of books, a few with ancient dust jackets, the rest with worn blue cloth covers. Nancy Drew.

An envelope lay on top of the books. Megan opened it and read the note Sylvie had written in her gently perfect handwriting:

"Dear Megan, Romy talked about how nice you'd been, letting her stay at the library. She mentioned how much you loved Nancy Drew. We think Romy would have wanted you to have these. Not for the library. For you. With gratitude, Sylvie and Wade."

Reverently, Megan ran her fingers across the spines of these decades-old books. She sorted through the spines until she found one with the title, *The Secret of the Old Clock*. She took it back to her balcony, sat on her favorite chair, and began to read.

Also by Pam Stucky:

A fast-paced, atmospheric whodunit that will keep you guessing until the end!

For two decades, the lush, isolated forests of the North Cascades have hidden a secret. Now, twenty years later, a mysterious contest has brought Mindy Harris back to the area she thought she'd left behind forever. A seemingly innocent creative design firm shows up for a company retreat, but all goes awry when one of their own turns up dead. Was it an accident? Murder? And how does the unsolved mystery from twenty years ago play into it all?

"A neat little mystery with the rare virtue that the setting and characters are as interesting as the unfolding story."

"A reflective tone, with heart and insight into human frailty and strength, made this a very worthwhile read."

connect

If you loved this book, tell your friends and let Pam know! Leave a review online, send a tweet to @pamstucky, and/or drop Pam a note at facebook.com/pamstuckyauthor.

Stay tuned for more! Be among the first to know when a new story is coming out by signing up for Pam's mailing list at pamstucky.com!

Visit pamstucky.com to find out more about Pam and her other fiction and non-fiction books.

acknowledgments

My gratitude to Skagit River Bald Eagle Interpretive Center for generously taking the time to answer my questions about eagles and eagle habitat in the Skagit River area.

Thank you to Chuck Perry, Kenmore Air pilot, for not running away when I asked, "Can we talk about ways a person might die in an airplane?" and for telling me about the dead stop carbon monoxide detector. Chuck also has ideas for writing his own mysteries. Get writing, Chuck!

As always, I am beyond grateful for those willing to give time and energy to offer critique and commentary on early drafts. Thank you to Donna Hostick and Beth Stucky who gave much helpful feedback and encouragement.

More by Pam Stucky

The Balky Point Adventures (MG/YA sci-fi)

"Aliens, infinite universes, ghosts AND time travel ... a winning literary combination if ever there was one." — *Just One More Chapter reviews*

This smart and unforgettable middle grade / young adult science fiction adventure series takes teens Emma, Charlie, Eve, and Ben, along with brilliant but quirky Dr. Waldo and a host of others, on adventures through time and space. Inspired the timeless wonder and fantasy of *A Wrinkle in Time*, with just a dash of *Doctor Who*, the Balky Point Adventures are for readers of all ages who love a good romp through the imaginative marvels of the universes, delivered with heart and wonder. Exciting and imaginative, courageous and thought-provoking, this series commends the strength of compassion, and the inherent power within each person to change the world ... or the universe.

Includes: *The Universes Inside the Lighthouse, The Secret of the Dark Galaxy Stone.*

The Wishing Rock series (contemporary fiction)

"It was just what the doctor ordered, fresh, quirky, funny in places and seasoned with wisdom. Light without being frivolous, it follows the story of a woman trying to find someone to fill her desire for true love and family." — *Tahlia Newland, author*

Wishing Rock, Washington, on Dogwinkle Island—don't look for it on a map; you won't find it there. The only place you can find this town is in your heart—and in the books in the Wishing Rock series!

The Wishing Rock books take us to the fictional town of Wishing Rock, in which all the town's residents live in the same building. In this *Northern Exposure*-esque slice-of-life series, letters between the neighbors and their friends chronicle the twists and turns of the characters' daily lives, and are interspersed with recipes tried and tested by the characters themselves. These novels, filled with wit, wisdom, and recipes, take characters on adventures far and near, and ultimately offer up insightful exploration of the ideas of community, relationships, happiness, hope, forgiveness, risk, trust, and love.

Includes: *Letters from Wishing Rock*, *The Wishing Rock Theory of Life*, and *The Tides of Wishing Rock* (all novels with recipes); *From the Wishing Rock Kitchens: Recipes from the Series* completes the series, with a compilation of all the recipes in the first three books.

The Pam on the Map series (travelogues)

"I couldn't resist reading the entire book, both for the wit and chuckles that I found on nearly every page, and to make sure I didn't miss any of the useful tips that were scattered throughout. I'm big on pre-trip research, and I found some tips in this book that I haven't seen elsewhere." — Emily, Amazon reader

In her Pam on the Map series, Pam sets out to discover and connect with people and places, and to take readers along on her adventures through her almost real-time reports. Raw and real, Pam's tales are infused with candid honesty, humorous observations, and perceptive insights. Pam's descriptive, entertaining, conversational style brings her trips alive, making readers feel as though they're traveling right along with her.

Though they're not guidebooks, the Pam on the Map books are still informative and illuminating, providing useful tips and plentiful ideas for people who might want to follow along in Pam's footsteps.

Includes: *Pam on the Map: Iceland*, *Pam on the Map: Seattle Day Trips*, *Pam on the Map (Retrospective): Ireland*, and *Pam on the Map (Retrospective): Switzerland*.